CAZAK

CONQUERED WORLD: BOOK SIXTEEN

ELIN WYN

CLOCK
WALK
PUBLISHING

SYBIL

"Three!" The entire crowd shouted with one voice.

"Two!" The energy in the room was electric, a thousand voices oiled by alcohol turning into a chorus. I let a smile spread across my lips as I focused on the holographic screen behind the DJ and held my flute of champagne up in the air.

"One!"

The whole crowd went nuts.

The retractable ceiling started sliding back to reveal a starry sky, and the whistle of a hundred fireworks climbing up into the night blended with the chorus. When the first fireworks went off, an explosion of light pushing away the darkness in the sky, I joined the others and cried out at the top of my lungs.

"Happy New Year!"

The room, which had its lights dimmed for the countdown, was now filled with the bright colors of the fireworks. They went on for almost ten minutes, covering the sky in colorful teardrops, and every single person in the club watched the show with a kind of wide-eyed amazement.

It had been a while since Kaster had seen such a celebration and, after a couple of rough years, I figured the entire city needed something like this.

I knew I did.

"Let's get this party started," the DJ screamed into his hovering microphone. He pushed a few buttons on his control panel and the holographic screen behind him lit up once more.

The neon colors there ebbed and flowed with a rhythm that matched the music, the pounding bass making my chest vibrate.

Placing my empty champagne flute on the counter, I headed onto the dance floor and brought both my hands up. Running my fingers through my hair, I swayed my hips to the rhythm. I whipped my hair back and forth, enjoying the vibrancy of the night, and let a wide smile take over my lips.

There was nothing better than a good party.

"Having fun?" Someone screamed into my ear, but I still had a hard time making out the words. I turned to see a handsome young man standing beside me, the sleeves of his white button-up shirt rolled up to his elbows.

He had the kind of grin that meant trouble, and there was a glint in his eyes that told me I had snagged all his attention.

"What?"

"Enjoying yourself, aren't you?" he repeated, and this time I replied with a wink. Facing him, I ran my hands down the sides of my body and dragged my teeth over my bottom lip.

I kept my eyes on his as I danced, and it didn't take long before he closed the distance between us. My father would've hated to see me dancing with a stranger, but what the hell.

Some dancing and innocent flirting never really killed anyone, right? No harm in living life and having some fun.

Even if, night after night, it felt like less fun.

But that wasn't a problem for right now.

At least, not a problem that couldn't be solved pretty easily.

"What do you say we grab some shots?" The guy screamed again, doing his best to talk over the loud music. He pointed toward the corner, where a group of five or six guys was busy downing shot after shot and I gave him a quick nod.

See? Problem solved.

Grabbing my hand, he led me across the packed dance floor and, somehow we managed to make our way to the place where his friends were. He motioned at the bartender for two shots and, just a couple of seconds later, I had a small glass pushed into my hands.

"Bottoms up!" I laughed and, without waiting for him, threw my head back and drank it all. I grimaced as the alcohol made its way down my throat, but I didn't let that stop me. Once another shot somehow appeared in front of me, I reached for it and drank it, too.

"Slow down," the man laughed. "You keep that up and you won't last the night."

"I can handle my liquor."

"I can see that."

"Are these your friends?" I asked him, pointing at the group of twenty-somethings surrounding him. He replied with a nod, and then started naming his friends. They all winked and nodded at me as my new friend introduced them all, but I wasn't really paying attention to any of it. I couldn't hear what their names were and, truth be told, I didn't really care.

All I wanted was to dance.

"Sure feels good, huh?"

"What does?" I asked him.

"Look around you," he smiled, waving at the crowd. "Notice anything?"

"Not really," I admitted.

"Not a single alien in here," he laughed. "I can't remember the last place I walked into without having to see one of them. Feels great, doesn't it?"

"I don't get it," I frowned. "Are you one of those anti-alien people?"

"Well, wouldn't you say that it's high time we—"

"I'm gonna dance," I cut him short and, without waiting for his reply, I turned my back on him and slipped back into the crowd.

It seemed like all everyone wanted to do nowadays was dabble in politics and talk smack about the aliens.

Why ruin a good party with such boring conversation?

"Who's your friend?" I heard someone laugh right behind me, and I spun on my heels, to see Aman, one of the girls that had come with me.

She was rocking back and forth on her heels, her eyes already turning glassy. Still, that didn't seem to stop her from sipping on whatever cocktail she had in her hand. "His friends are cute. Care to introduce me?"

"Nah," I laughed back at her. "They're boring as hell."

"Really?"

"They just wanna talk about aliens and whatever."

"Ugh." Rolling her eyes, she shook her head. "Let's get out of here then, before this entire party turns into a snooze fest. I know of a club just around the block, and a friend of mine told me they're partying hard in there."

"What are you waiting for?" I grinned. "Lead the way."

We stumbled onto the streets a few minutes later, the chaos of a New Year's celebration punctuated by loud chants and the laughter of people drinking outside the bars. I followed after Aman as best I could, but it didn't take a genius to see that I would have to put an end to my night.

I was already swaying like a boat during a storm, and the world around me seemed to be spinning too fast for my eyes to keep up.

"You go ahead," I finally said, hands on my knees as I tried to catch my breath. "I think I'm gonna call it a night."

"It's not even two," Aman protested, but I just gave her a sheepish smile. "C'mon, you're not gonna leave me alone, are you? I can't handle all the cute boys by myself, can I?"

"I'm sure you'll manage." Standing straight—at least as much as I could—I ran one hand through my hair and scanned my surroundings, trying to remember where I had left the car. "I think I've just drunk too much."

"You're a disappointment, Sybil," Aman laughed. "C'mon, I'll walk you to your car."

The two of us went along a side avenue, and it didn't take long before I spotted the turquoise sports aircar parked in front of a club. I unlocked the door with my fingerprint, and then climbed awkwardly inside. Sprawled in the back seat, I waved Aman goodbye and told the computer to close the door.

"Take me home," I said, doing my best not to spill dinner all over the leather upholstery. My dad would kill me if that happened.

Probably.

He frowned at everything I did, but whenever I tried to change, take some classes, move out, maybe find a job, he'd been just as dismissive.

I knew he missed mom, but he couldn't pretend nothing had changed.

"Destination set as: home," the car's AI droned in its monotone voice, and the engine came alive with a growl. "Estimated arrival time: 25 minutes." I bounced in my seat as the car pushed its weight off the pavement, and I quickly buckled myself up.

I spent the entire journey with my eyes closed, and I only dared to open them when I became certain dinner would remain in my stomach. I looked out the window to see the quiet suburbs underneath me, the brightly lit center of Kaster just a flash in the distance, and I rested my forehead against the glass.

A few minutes later, the car started its descent into

the gated courtyard of a stately manor. It stopped right in front of the imperial staircase that led the way to the front entrance, and I jumped out of the car as silently as cat.

A very drunk cat. Even though I was pretty sure someone must've heard the car, I still hoped I'd manage to get inside my bedroom without anyone noticing me.

I held my breath as I opened the front door, but my father's voice immediately boomed from the entrance hall. "Do you have any idea what time it is?" He stood just a few steps away from the door, both hands on his hips as he stared me down.

He was wearing a tailored suit that somehow managed to hide the weight he had put on these last few years, an outfit he must've chosen for whatever boring party he'd had to attend.

You'd think that the mayor of Kaster would be livin' it up, but that wasn't the case.

It was never the case.

More often than not, all my father had to do was go to infinite administrative meetings and attend functions so boring I could fall asleep just thinking of them.

"It's...uh...two in the morning," I mumbled, trying to pretend I was sober.

It didn't work. Every word I tried to push out of my

mouth was as mellow as a caramel that had been left under a summer sun.

"Are you drunk?"

"It's New Year's," I said. "I've had a few drinks. So what?"

He didn't say anything. He just stared at me, eyes narrowed, and clenched his fists. He started to shout at me, but I was so damn drunk I couldn't understand a word of what he was saying.

"I'm going to bed," I merely said, and turned my back on him. He kept on shouting as I stumbled up the stairs that led to my bedroom, but I just ignored him.

There was something odd about him. Even though he didn't really like my partying habits, my father wasn't really the kind of man to act as angrily as he was right now.

Whatever.

Stepping into my bedroom, I made a beeline straight toward my bed and collapsed on top of the covers.

I was so drunk I didn't even fall asleep.

I straight up passed out.

CAZAK

I enjoyed working the night shift. It was quiet, simple, peaceful, and the best time for me to sit back and think. The night shift was a great chance for me to get away from the insanity and the stress of the day-to-day comings and goings of my job.

Of course, ever since the Xathi were defeated, our jobs had changed. We were no longer strike teams being sent out to conduct covert acts against our enemies. We were now being used for supply runs, security work, and the occasional protection details for whoever might need it.

Like tonight.

Tonight, Jalok, Navat, and I were on security detail, helping the local police force maintain sanity during the New Year's celebrations.

I liked New Year's celebrations. They were always a time to throw worries and concerns to the side, at least for an evening, and celebrate the end of an old year and the beginning of a new one that would hopefully be an improvement over the previous.

Then again, it was also a time to throw inhibitions and willpower on the back burner in order to enjoy one evening of fun, debauchery, and insanity.

As long as you maintained a semblance of control over your actions. I used to be one of those people that would lose control and just focus strictly on the fun and debauchery.

It had cost me.

However, after a life-changing moment, followed immediately by a universe-changing moment, I was no longer that person and I was now the one that tried to help control and save the people that lost control.

That's what we were working on tonight, trying to control insanity.

"Cazak, we got a call," Jalok, my cousin, said as he clicked off his communicator with the police. "They want us at a party near some place called Leverage Tower. While it's not out of hand yet, they're worried that it will be soon, so they want us there to help keep an eye on things."

"Okay, let's go watch people dance in the snow," Navat said with a smile. I turned my head up for a moment and watched as the snow fell through the lights.

Dancing in this would have been fun in my younger days. Of course, humans were the only ones that held their New Year's celebrations in the middle of winter, the rest of the sane universe held theirs either during spring or just before the summer equinox.

"Drive or jog?" I asked as I turned my head back to the others.

"Jog, it's not far from here," Jalok smiled. He started jogging, Navat and I only a few paces behind. The city was unnaturally beautiful with the holiday decorations, the snow, and the lights. The revelers that were walking and dancing in the streets stayed away from us.

As we jogged, Jalok put his hand up to his ear and spoke to someone. I couldn't hear his words, but when he started jerking his head around in anger, I got the gist of the conversation. "Move it, people are starting to argue and there's some minor physical activity. They're worried it's gonna turn into a fight and we need to get there, now."

We picked up our pace, turning our jog into a run, but not quite a sprint. We were at Leverage Tower within six minutes. As we arrived, there was a small scuffle happening between two groups of partygoers, and I could hear their argument from where we were.

"You fucking alien-lover! You're probably pregnant

with one of their spawn, aren't you?" The speaker was a large man, not muscular, and he was picking on a young lady, yelling at her. When her date, or just someone trying to help her, stepped forward, the large man pushed him.

I stepped forward and he turned to me.

"Yeah, you, you alien dumb fuck," he growled as he pointed at me. "I asked, what the hell are you looking at? You staring at one of *our* women? You thinking of taking one of *our* women? What, you think we're here to serve you, to get down on our knees and bow down to you?"

"Don't respond," Jalok said quietly. "Let's not provoke them." Then he turned to the crowd. "We're not here for any trouble. We're simply here to ensure that everyone has a good time without anything untoward happening."

"Go fuck yourself," the loud man yelled. He was a young one, possibly mid-twenties, if that. He was dressed very well, with a bright green shirt, dark gray vest, gray tie, and gray slacks. It was an impressive ensemble. Too bad the clothes were filled with an idiot with a big mouth.

"I'm going to apologize for my friend here," I said as I took a step forward. "He forgot to mention that we're working with the local police force and that we have jurisdictional rights to arrest anyone causing trouble.

Now, we're simply here to ensure that everyone has a good time and that no one does anything to mess up said good time. Let's simply leave it at that, shall we?"

The human rolled his eyes and stumbled a bit to one side. His friends laughed, but one of them leaned into his ear and started talking, pointing at us. "I know, shut up," Green Shirt snarled. He turned his attention back to us. "It's simple, alien bitch, get the hell off our planet."

"Come on, man. Leave him alone," another one of the men said.

"Shut the fuck up, Eric, or I'll stick your head up his alien ass. You know what? Screw this." Then Green Shirt started walking towards us, almost stomping.

"Don't do this," I said. "It's not going to end well for you."

He was only a few paces away, snarling. His eyes flashed and I knew right then that he was being taken over.

"He's possessed," I warned the others as they raised their weapons.

I, instead, let go of mine and let it swing on its strap behind me. "Don't do this," I repeated. "I really don't want to hurt you. Just go back to the party and celebrate."

I stepped a few steps forward, my hands held out to my side, palms out.

That didn't calm him down as I'd wanted. Instead, it seemed to infuriate him more. He got within swinging distance and threw a left hook. It was an easy blow to block, as he was off-balance, and in his inebriated state, he didn't have the power that he would have had if it was simply anger driving him.

So, I blocked it and pushed him away. His eyes went wide and he charged me. He tried to tackle me, but I grabbed him, caught his shoulders, spun him around, and pushed him away again. "Please stop. I warned you that this was not going to go well for you." I turned back to Jalok and Navat. "When are the police getting here?"

Jalok shrugged.

"Great." I turned back to Green Shirt. He rushed me again. This time, instead of trying to tackle me, he jumped into the air, his knee aimed at my face. I caught him, but his knee connected with my shoulder, driving me off balance as I held him and tried to throw him off me. Instead of merely throwing him off to the side, as I'd intended, he was thrown against a trash can. When he shouted out in pain, his friends yelled in anger and rushed us.

"Rek, Cazak. What did you do?" Navat cursed as he slung his weapon behind him and caught his attacker. Jalok sidestepped his and threw a quick punch to the back of his head.

I shook my own head and turned back towards Green Shirt. He charged again, but this time, he actually caught me off guard.

He feinted to my left, then went to my right, except he went low instead of high like I had been expecting. He caught me in the knee, dragging me down to the ground. He jumped on top of me and started throwing punches. I managed to cover up and block most of them, then I reached out, caught a punch, and put him into an armbar.

I pulled and snapped my head up, headbutting him. I rolled him over, pulling his arm behind him, and there was a sickening pop from his shoulder.

At his scream, I let go and reached behind me for the handcuffs the police had given us. I snapped them onto one wrist, then onto the other, then looked, up to see Jalok and Navat standing, their weapons pointed at the rabble rousers, and the police finally arriving.

Statements were taken, the three men were taken away, and I was double checked to make sure my knee was fine.

"That was fun," Navat said with a smile.

I let out a bark of laughter, making the others look at me with arched eyebrows. "What?"

"You thought that was fun? I was being sarcastic," Navat said.

I shrugged. "Eh. The night has only just begun.

Maybe we'll get to see some more nice cars, or another idiot in nice clothes being possessed."

I knew I wasn't acting like myself, but that's why I loved the night shift.

Nothing was normal.

SYBIL

I woke up feeling like a vampire. The sunlight streaming through the large windows of my bedroom made my head throb violently, and a wave of nausea flowed over me as I sat up on the bed. Pinching the bridge of my nose, I sucked in a deep breath and forced my eyelids open.

God, what a hangover.

Groaning, I swung my legs off the bed and walked toward the windows. The sky was a deep gray, and the courtyard was covered in at least two feet of snow. It was a lovely sight, except the brightness of it all didn't help the throbbing in my head. I drew the curtains, momentarily relishing the shadows that embraced me, and ambled toward my ensuite bathroom.

I stared into the mirror. My skin had a grayish cast

to it and my eyes looked hollow. "I can't keep doing this."

But at the moment, I couldn't figure out what else to do. Coffee first, then a plan.

Two minutes later, a fine mist started taking over the bathroom, and only then did I push my dress down my body and onto the floor. Naked, I stepped inside the shower and threw my head back as the warm water fell against my skin.

There was nothing better than a hot shower after a late night of partying. Now I just needed to munch on some toast, drink a cup or two of coffee, and I'd be good to go. With some luck, I wouldn't even have to take an aspirin.

"Computer, what's the time?" I asked, and the AI system that was part of the manor immediately spoke up in a warm feminine voice.

"It's half past seven in the morning."

It was early then. I tended to get up after lunch whenever I spent the whole night drinking, but it seemed like my body was ready to tackle the first day of the new year on a high note.

Not that I had much to do.

My father was always needling me to find something productive to do, but I felt like I was already productive enough. At least when it came to partying.

Feeling better now, I toweled myself off and put on

a pair of ripped jeans and a trendy sweater. I applied some light makeup, checked my reflection in the mirror, then took a deep breath before leaving the room.

A maid was already making the rounds, changing linens in one of the guest rooms, and from downstairs came the bright sound of cutlery hitting the porcelain of a plate. It seemed like I wasn't the only one up this early on New Year's Day.

"Up already?" My father asked me, one eyebrow cocked as he saw me come down the stairs. He sat at the large dining table all by himself, a plate with fried bacon and scrambled eggs in front of him. "How are you feeling?"

"I'm fine."

"Fine, huh?" He echoed, a smirk on his lips. "Are you going to tell me you don't have a hangover?"

"Dad, I already told you," I sighed. "I had a couple of drinks last night. I mean, it was New Year's Eve. What's the harm in it?"

"There's no harm in a little celebrating, Sybil. Thing is, I think you're overdoing it. You're out partying and drinking almost every night of the week. Don't you think enough is enough?"

"Come on, Dad." Sitting on one of the chairs beside him, I gave the butler a little smile as he quickly placed a plate similar to my father's in front of me. "I think that's my cue. Don't you think last night was enough? Or are you going to lose it again?"

"Last night?" he asked me, furrowing his brow. "What are you talking about, Sybil?"

"You shouted at me." I raised an eyebrow. "Blew your stack."

"I did what?" He shook his head. "I know we've talked about this before, but I never lose my temper with you."

"Apparently last night was the first time, then." If I sounded annoyed, that's because I was. Sure, I came home completely drunk, but it seemed like my father had had a few drinks himself. How could he not remember the way he had shouted at me? "Were you drunk last night, or something? That would be ironic."

"I didn't have anything to drink," he insisted. "Seriously, I have no idea what you're talking about."

"Whatever." Rolling my eyes, I finished the food on my plate and pushed my chair back. I was about to march out of the house when I suddenly felt guilty about the way I was acting.

He tried. I knew he did. Sometimes, between running the city and trying to pretend nothing had changed since mom died, he must just get exhausted. Maybe he'd cracked a little. That didn't make him a bad guy.

I turned on my heels and walked toward my father. Leaning into him, I kissed his cheek. "I love you, Dad."

"And I love you, Sybil," he replied, sounding more tired than I ever remembered him to be. He looked up at me, managed a weak smile, and then returned his attention to his breakfast. Not knowing what else to do, I headed out of the house and got inside the car.

"Take me to Hops," I told the AI, and soon enough the mayor's mansion was nothing but a small dot in the scenery.

A few miles ahead of the car, the tall buildings that occupied most of Kaster's city center rose like snowcapped mountains. It would have been a beautiful New Year's Day, but it was hard to feel excited about...well, about anything.

I thought of my father, alone in a house big enough for God knows how many families, and I thought of my mother. Life had been so much easier when the three of us were a family. After she passed away, it was like a permanent fog had settled over my life.

It was hard to get up much energy for anything, much less getting myself out of the rut I'd fallen into.

"We've arrived at the destination," the AI droned half an hour later as it settled into a vacant spot at the skyport. The door slid open silently and I stepped outside, the warmth of the mall immediately making me regret my decision to bring a sweater.

The girls were already there, standing in front of Hops, the coffee shop where we usually gathered to gossip and cure our hangovers.

"How are you doing? Brain still foggy?" Aman laughed, and I just gave her a shrug. She had bags under her eyes, and her makeup was all wrong. Her hair was slightly disheveled, as well, and she sounded as if she was exhausted.

"At least I got some sleep," I laughed with her. "You haven't even gone to bed, have you?"

"Is it that obvious?" She grimaced, and the other three girls just rolled their eyes. Even though they weren't what I'd call close friends, this small group had been a constant in my life ever since my mother's passing. Whenever there was a party, they were always there, and they made sure to drag me along for the ride.

Once upon a time, the noise and the never-ending partying had been my lifeline. Now, I wasn't so sure.

Together, we stepped inside the two-story coffee house and settled down at a large table by the corner, one that gave us a panoramic view of the city below. We used the touchscreen on the table to make our orders, and soon enough a waiter appeared with five coffees on a tray, our names scribbled on the cups.

"Have I told you that Sybil ditched an entire group of guys last night?" Aman said in a conspiratorial tone, and the other girls just raised their eyebrows at me. "I'm dead serious. They were buying her shots, crazy with the way she was dancing, and she just blew them off. They were cute, too."

"Oh my God," Lisandre said, her accent making it obvious to anyone within earshot that she had been born and bred in Nyheim. "What's up with you, Sybil? You're such a tease. You gotta move past the flirting."

"The fun is in the flirting," I said with a laugh. I had always been a nice quiet girl and, even though I had grown accustomed to all the partying, I wasn't as crazy about men as the four of them were.

Sure, I enjoyed all the dancing and flirting, but that was it.

None of the men I came across in the nightclubs or bars seemed to hold my interest for more than a couple of minutes. I wasn't exactly a prude, but I had my limits.

Maybe I was just picky.

Thankfully, the conversation drifted away from me after a few more laughs. Aman was recounting how she had met a guy in the last club she had gone to, and she had spent the night at his place. After a wild night of drinking and dancing between the sheets, she had rolled out of bed just so she could meet us for coffee.

As the girls talked and laughed, I stared out the window and watched the snowflakes slowly drift past me. I thought back to my conversation with my father, and sighed.

I knew I couldn't go on like this forever, partying every single night and trying to ignore the fact that I was now an adult, but I didn't really know how to change things.

The drinking, the dancing, and the partying...those things kept me distracted from all the things I didn't want to face.

I had lost my mother, my relationship with my father had seen better days, and I had absolutely no sense of purpose. It was hard to feel motivated about anything with all those things weighing me down.

I wanted to be a better woman, no doubt about it.

I just didn't know how to go about it.

"Oh my God," Lisandre snorted, discreetly pointing somewhere behind me. "Can you believe that?"

I turned in my chair, to see a small girl of about five pestering a tall Valorni. He was hunched over a table in the corner, quietly drinking from a tall cup of coffee, and the young girl seemed fascinated by the alien's size.

She was peppering him with a thousand questions and, even though he was enormous in size, he was patiently answering her, a wide smile on his lips. The kid's parents watched from a table to the side, amused with the situation.

"What about it?" I asked Lisandre, and she just cocked one eyebrow up.

"Are you serious? Like, her parents are completely

irresponsible, don't you think? They're letting a kid talk to one of those monsters. Like, if I had a kid, I would never let her alone with one of them, that much I can tell you."

The other girls nodded their agreement, and I just looked at them, not knowing what to say.

"Please don't tell me you're into that anti-alien stuff, as well," I finally breathed out. "Don't you have anything more important to think about?"

"That is important," Lisandre insisted. "My father tells me those things are taking our jobs, and God knows what else they might be planning to do. I mean, they handle a lot of security in the city. Doesn't it make you feel like you're a prisoner?"

"That's so stupid," I snapped. "Do you really think those guys want to hurt us? Just take a look at them. If they wanted to, they could've taken over all our cities already. And have you forgotten they were the ones stopping Kaster from being turned into a pile of rubble during the war?"

I shook my head then, more to myself than to them, and found myself going up to my feet. "You know what? I think I'm going home."

They called my name as I walked out of the coffee shop, but I just ignored them. My headache was slowly returning, and I was in no mood to discuss the sociological implications of having aliens in our cities.

If I wanted to be bored out of my mind, I could've stayed home with my father.

Besides, why the hell were people so obsessed with the damn aliens?

Sure, they looked scary as hell, but all they seemed to want was a regular life.

That was a curious thought: those aliens wanted the exact same thing I did.

Maybe I had more in common with them than with my group of my so-called friends.

CAZAK

Kaster was a beautiful city on the coast. When you got a chance to sit at the beach and watch the waves crash as the snow was falling, it's one of the most amazing sights I could have ever imagined.

Staying here would be something I could see myself doing, if I was inclined to retire and if I was certain that staying here would be worth it.

Beauty was not enough to keep me, at least not by itself.

It was the new year and things were the same as the old year.

We still had humans standing against us, trying to drive us away.

The irony was that if we could leave, most of us would be gone in a heartbeat.

Amusingly, they also wanted the Puppet Master gone. That was something that couldn't happen. If he tried to leave, he would have to break the planet in half in order to do so.

Less amusingly, we now had these Ancient Enemies of the Puppet Master's that were taking over humans and turning them against us.

Friends, people we knew, people we trusted, any of them could be turned at any moment and become an enemy, literally in an instant.

But we still had humans standing with us, helping us and guiding us through the intricacies of this world and the people that lived on it.

Ankau was a planet of mystery, wonder, beauty, friendship, and things that could make even the sourest of people smile.

And Kaster was one of those things.

I did not want to leave it, not yet, but orders had come in. We were needed back in Sauma for supplies to be transferred to Nyheim which would then be brought by another team to the new settlement of Aramita.

These new settlements were popping up everywhere. People trying to find homes and places to live that were away from where the Xathi had landed and devastated, away from where we were, or away from where the Puppet Master was known to regularly operate.

Aramita was on the northern coastline, so they would have cooler temperatures and the beaches were different, rockier, with less sand. It also meant better fishing. Aramita was building itself up to be a fishing mecca, or at least the beginnings of one.

I let out a deep breath, took one last look at the beaches of Kaster, and turned away. I walked to my small hover bike that I had rented, got on, and started it up.

As it lifted itself into the air, I fought to maintain balance. The rekking thing kept trying to tip to the right for the first few seconds before balancing itself out.

As soon as it was balanced, I threw it into gear and rode through the city streets all the way to the airfield where Jalok and Navat were waiting for me.

"Anything to get out of loading the shuttle, huh?" Navat said with a shake of his head as he carried a box into the shuttle.

"What? I didn't know we were supposed to be loading things up. I thought they were doing that?" I answered, pointing at the human workers two bay doors down, loading another shuttle.

"They had a call to load medical supplies for Glymna," Jalok grunted as he picked up a box, then motioned for me to get over there and help out. "So, we're loading."

I walked over and picked up a box. I ended up grunting a bit, too, it was heavy. Jalok and Navat chuckled a bit. "So, see what you wanted to see about human celebrations?" Navat asked.

"What do you mean?"

"We both saw how you were looking at the human women the other night."

I rolled my eyes. "You two are idiots. I love you, but you're idiots. I won't deny that human women are attractive. But it would never work."

"Seriously?"

"Yes, seriously," I said back as I helped Jalok pick up a larger crate. "You two do realize that most of our work has been war, and when we ended said war, we were immediately thrown into another one. Don't you? Humans aren't meant for the life of war as we know it."

"Pick your end up higher, damn it," Jalok cursed, slipping into using human curses as he struggled to hold up his part of the crate's weight.

"Apologies." I lifted my end of the crate, better distributing the weight between us.

"And, yes," Jalok groaned. "We do realize that. Are you done getting your 'serenity' now?"

I nodded as we set the crate down.

"Good. Now, let's get these to Sauma, pick up the new stuff, and get to Nyheim. Okay?"

"Okay." We finished loading the supplies and flew to

Sauma. The jungle looked different from the air, especially covered in snow. "Coming down," I said as I brought us in for a landing.

"Let's try to get this stuff unloaded quickly, I want to get back home," Jalok said.

"You just want to get back to Dottie, now that she's moved to Nyheim to be near you," Navat teased.

"Shut up."

We laughed and joked with one another for the next hour as we unloaded things meant for Sauma and reloaded things meant to go to Nyheim and Aramita.

We flew back to Nyheim, landing not at the airfield, but in the lot of one of the warehouses.

"Hey, what the hell are you guys doing? You can't land here," one of the workers was yelling as he came running out. "Goddammit, should have figured it was you three morons."

"Hello to you, too, Dent," Navat smiled as we stepped off the shuttle. "What, you don't like front door service to make your life easier?"

Dent threw his arms up. "You're supposed to park in the back if you're going to do this skrell. Now I need to redirect everything through the warehouse."

"Oh, boohoo."

I held back my laughter as I turned my head away. Navat and Dent were always messing with one another. "Hey, do you need me?" I asked Jalok.

"No, we're good. Dent is in charge now and Navat is doing his best to piss him off. It's what they do. I think the humans call it something stupid like a 'bromance,' or something idiotic like that. Go, you're off duty."

"Thank you."

I took off, jogging for the armory. The people of Nyheim still had the winter decorations up. The tradition, we had learned, came from old Earth. While the actual holidays were no longer relevant, the people were always happy to have a reason for a good party.

And with the decorations was the snow. The rest of the team had already gotten over the snow and were close to being tired of it, or sick and tired of it.

Sk'lar was almost on the verge of hating the snow, but that might have had something to do with him slipping on a patch of ice hidden under the snow and bruising his tailbone. The nonstop teasing from the rest of us when he struggled to sit, or stand, probably didn't help, either.

Me?

I loved the snow. It was beautiful, peaceful, and delicate. The artistry of the snowflake was a magnificent thing, unable to be duplicated without losing the soul of the artwork. Then, when you put it all together into something as simple as a snowball, or a 'snowman', the creation was extended into something completely different

After dropping off my gear, I jogged over to the children's clinic a few blocks away from the armory. This was what I was really looking forward to when I came back to Nyheim.

These children were all dealing with various illnesses that the local doctors were still unable to find a cure for.

I wasn't a doctor, but spending time with them was something that I could do to try to make their days better.

And children were less afraid of the 'big bad aliens' than the adults were. They were much more willing to hang out with me, even with my deformity.

Years ago, during one of my wilder nights, I had gotten into a fight with a drunk, thinking I could handle him easily.

Unfortunately, I had been wrong. The fight ended with me in infirmary, my left ear missing, and a long cut from my ear to my mouth. Now, that cut was a long scar and my left ear was missing.

Luckily, these children didn't care about that.

"Cazak!" a few of them called out, their smiling faces making me so much happier than I had been at the beach.

Seeing their faces was the highlight of my day, better than anything else that I could ever see.

The kids didn't care about my ear, or lack thereof.

They didn't care that my skin was red and scaled, or that I'd been born too far away to even explain.

They cared that I played with them, brought them what presents I could, and visited every chance I got.

And the parents and staff cared, because I was good at research, and had started to look up symptoms of what these children went through, comparing them to similar illnesses throughout the Valorni, Skotan, K'ver and Urai databases.

So far, while I hadn't found any cures, I had found a couple of ways to make things easier for some of these children.

"So," I said with a clap of my hands after hugging all of the kids. "Who wants to build snowmen and have a snowball fight? And for those of you that can't, who wants to, anyway?"

The kids cheered.

I smiled.

Life was good.

SYBIL

I woke up with a start.

It was another evening. I must have slept through the whole day again.

It probably made sense, given that I was out all night.

Then I remembered the previous morning. I'd snapped at my friends. I just couldn't stand to see them acting so horribly to the people who had saved us.

My face scrunched in anger. The hell with them. They shouldn't have acted like that. I figured I was rich, young, and the mayor's daughter. I could always find new friends if they wanted to hold a grudge.

When I finally dragged myself out of bed and got dressed, it was nearing the time my father usually came home.

I wasn't exactly looking forward to it, but headed downstairs to our main floor and drank a cup of coffee, so I could at least be somewhat awake when he arrived.

The front door opened, and I headed into the foyer to greet my father. He came inside, and stared at me with a blank expression. All he did was blink for what seemed like an eternity.

"Uh, hello, Dad." I waved at him in mock sincerity.

He continued to stare for several more seconds before speaking.

"Hello, daughter." His voice seemed oddly hollow, as if he were reading mechanical instructions rather than greeting his only child.

"Daughter?" I mean, yes, technically that was a correct description of my relationship to him.

But he'd never called me that before, not in that tone.

I narrowed my gaze at him. "Did you have a rough day at the office, or something?"

My father blinked a few more times, then spoke in the same monotone.

"Or something."

Right. Time to get out of here, get to anywhere at all.

"Okay. I'm heading over to the Landing tonight, so don't wait up."

I rushed up the stairs before he could begin to

lecture me. From what I could hear on the second floor, he just stood in the parlor without moving.

He didn't take off his coat and hang it up or head into the kitchen for a quick snack, which was his usual routine after work. My father remained still as a stone the whole time I was getting ready.

Trying to ignore his strange behavior, I picked out a black fringed dress that was so short I wore opaque hose beneath it, just in case I got a little energetic on the dance floor. Next, I pulled my hair back and up into an elaborate braid, the whole time straining my ears to see if my father had moved in the slightest.

As near as I could tell, he had not.

I finished my look with a pair of dangly ruby pendant earrings that my father had given me at Yuletide. Then I slipped on a pair of shoes that, while sexy, had low enough heels I could still dance in them, and headed downstairs.

I found my father right where I had left him. After giving him an incredulous look, I attempted to walk around him and head out the front door.

"Well, I'm leaving. Don't bother waiting up."

"Where are you going?"

I was taken aback by the ferocity in my father's tone. Even when he'd been angry with me in the past, he never shouted like that.

"To the Landing, for a party, I just told you—"

"You're doing no such thing, daughter. Look at how you're dressed. You look like a slut."

"What?" My cheeks burned. Never before had my father called me something like that. Spoiled and entitled, maybe, but never a slut. "You bought me this dress."

"I bought everything here, you spoiled brat. You're living off my labor."

"I'm not going to stand here and listen to you scream at me." I walked around him and put my hand on the doorknob. Suddenly his hand clasped my wrist. "What are you doing?"

"You're not going anywhere." I tried to fight him, but his grip was surprisingly strong. Not only could I not budge his hand from my wrist, but he pulled my arm up in the air away, from the doorknob.

"Daddy, you're hurting me."

He had no response except to turn around and half drag me through the house. Stumbling in my heels, I struggled to keep up as he took me into the living room. When did my father get so strong?

With a snarl, he hurled me onto the sofa.

"You are a most disappointing offspring." His face was a mask of rage, but his words and tone seemed oddly precise. "I labor all day to provide for your upbringing, and all you do is lie about and contribute nothing. You are a waste of resources and matter, and I am ashamed to be your father."

"Daddy?" I couldn't believe what I was hearing.

Sure, he been acting odd when I came home on New Year's, but now he'd taken it to a whole new level. "Have you, have you been drinking? Do you have a headache?"

I was grasping at straws, looking for some way to explain my father's odd speech and behavior. He really didn't act like he'd been drinking, but it was all I could come up with.

"I have imbibed caffeinated beverages and water. You will imbibe my words, daughter, and stop behaving like a member of the monarchy, and more like an obedient offspring."

My wrist ached terribly from where he'd grabbed and dragged me across the house.

His face shone with sweat, though the living space had a lot of windows and was frequently chilly, as it was that evening.

I began to wonder if perhaps he were coming down with a virus, when he snapped again.

"Just the sight of you disgusts me. You're spoiled and revolting."

I shrank from the sight of his fury, confused by his strange speech and manner. My father, a man to whom I could look for comfort and security, even if he were angry with me, loomed over me like an angry titan. Never before had I seen him so consumed by indignant anger.

Just when I began to fear that my father would actually physically strike me, he abruptly changed again. The rage drained from his face, replaced by the original blank expression he'd worn when he came through the door.

He turned away from me and walked, quite calmly, into the kitchen. I heard cabinets opening and him rummaging around in them.

"What do you want for dinner, daughter?"

I was flabbergasted, utterly discombobulated. A moment before, he'd been the portrait of pure, mad rage, and now he seemed utterly placid.

Once upon a time I'd thought about being a nurse, had done a little bit of reading, before my father had decided that I needed to stay home to be a hostess for him.

From what I remembered of my reading, such a rapid shift in moods was usually the product of drugs, or mental illness, but there was no history of either in our family.

"What do you want for dinner?"

His voice came again, still calm but with an insistent edge. I stammered out something, I don't even remember what, and then I gingerly rose to my feet.

Checking on his position the whole time, I crept through the living space and moved with as much stealth as I could muster up the stairs.

Once I reached my room, I shut the door tightly, then locked it after a moment's thought.

Then I curled up on my bed, my back against the headboard. I hugged my knees and buried my face in between them, sobbing in helpless fear.

What had happened to my father?

CAZAK

The guys were getting tired of my constant admiration of the snow, but I didn't care. Snow was possibly my favorite weather phenomenon.

It was something that we didn't get to enjoy as much back at home. Skotans occasionally left a few fields and parks filled with snow so the children could experience it, or so we could train in it, but it usually melted away too quickly to enjoy.

Here, the humans left the snow where it fell. They moved it off the streets and the sidewalks, but generally, humans enjoyed the snow and had fun with it.

So, instead of letting me do patrols with them or help them on some of the reconstruction projects, I was told to go do what I wanted to do, so I was spending my day with the kids and their parents.

At least until lunch, when Jalok called me.

"What's going on, cousin?" I asked, as I held off a small mob of little fingers, determined this time to find the ticklish spot under my scales.

"I need you to come with me and Dottie back to Kaster. I've already cleared it with Sk'lar and the general."

"Okay. Not to sound repetitive, though, but what's going on?"

I could hear him sigh into the comm and I could hear the frustration in his voice.

He hated it when I questioned a request or an order from him.

He always thought he was second-in-command of the team, and we didn't really argue the point simply because the rest of us didn't want the responsibility.

"Dottie received a call from her friend Sybil. Sybil thinks there's something wrong with her father and Dottie is thinking it might be a possession. The symptoms and description sound right."

"When do we go?"

"As soon as you get to the airfield. Dottie and I are headed there now."

"Okay. I'll meet you there. Standard load from the armory or full gear?"

"Standard load. We're not trying to scare people and create a situation. Oh, minor note. Sybil's father is the mayor."

"Great. Thanks. See you there." I turned off the comm and looked over at the children. "I'm sorry, guys. I have to go to work."

"No." "Why?" "Please stay."

"I don't want you to go." "Oh, come on."

I did my best to hold my laughter in check because it was funny, it was cute, and it really felt good to have them want me around. "I'm sorry. I really want to stay, you know that. But I have to go help someone."

After another minute or two of saying goodbye and receiving hugs, I was finally on my way. I had to wait a little while for Jalok and Dottie to arrive, but it was long enough for me to get my armor on and make sure my weapons were properly loaded.

"You got here fast," Jalok commented with a grin.

"Well, since you said this was just a business trip, I just grabbed my spare suit from here."

"You actually store your armor here?"

"Not *my* armor, per se, but a spare that I borrowed from someone," I answered, turning my head away from my cousin as I answered.

"Oh, you son of a three-titted markant. That's where my extra set of armor disappeared to, you bastard." Luckily, his voice was filled more with humor than rage, so I wasn't worried about any sort of retaliation. "What happened to your spare?"

"I'm using my spare as my primary. My original primary armor was destroyed when the *Vengeance* blew up. I've been using my spare set ever since."

"Why haven't you requisitioned another set?"

"Keeps slipping my mind. Are we going, or standing here all day to talk?"

"He's right, we need to go. Hi, Cazak," Dottie said as she walked past us towards the shuttle.

"Hey, Dottie."

"Let's move, boys."

Jalok and I looked at one another, shared a smile, and said in union, "Yes, ma'am." Then, as we chuckled a bit to ourselves, we joined her on the shuttle.

"You boys talk too damn much, you know that?"

"What? We're just staying in communication, that's all," I explained, the smile on my face as big and non-creepy as I could make it. She smiled in return and shook her head as she turned to Jalok.

"He thinks he's funny, doesn't he?"

My cousin shrugged. "He tries. He's a lot less serious than me or Sk'lar, but not quite the funny man as Tyehn or Sakev."

"Oh, so he's one of those lighthearted serious guys then." It wasn't a question, it was her making a statement of how she saw me. I couldn't argue, really.

Jalok shrugged. "To a point, yes."

I started whistling as I launched the shuttle, getting us into the air and flying towards Kaster.

"Aww, he doesn't like us talking about him," Dottie mocked playfully.

I looked back. "It doesn't bother me as much as you think. Just figured I'd let the two of you converse since, according to my cousin there, you don't talk much when you're around each other. I mean, there are noises but no conversation."

Her squeal and the slapping sound that quickly came from behind me were music to my ear.

For the next few minutes, I heard Jalok trying to explain to Dottie that I was lying - I was, and that he didn't talk to me about their sex life- he didn't, usually.

But cousins are for teasing, right?

Eventually, we landed in Kaster, where Dottie already had a car waiting for us. We got in, she gave directions, and we were on our way.

Authorities had discreetly been putting out the word that if people saw something strange, they should report it.

So I had no way of knowing if what we were walking into was something serious or someone being trigger-happy with their emergency comms.

A byproduct of the Xathi war and the hybrids that had been created was to make people ever fearful that their family, friends, and neighbors were switching into mindless automatons.

Once Command figured out how to explain the Ancient Enemies and their ability to possess humans to the general population, everyone would report their neighbors for looking at them sideways.

Ten minutes and a few dozen turns later, we were dropped off at the mayor's house, where Sybil met us at the door.

Her gray eyes were different than any other I had ever seen. They radiated and sparkled with a light that I had never seen before.

But right now, all that sparkle was overwhelmed by worry. I could read the fear on her face, in her eyes. She was absolutely terrified, but she shifted her attention back to Dottie.

"Oh my god, thank you for coming. Thank you," she said as she threw her arms around Dottie and drew her in for a huge hug.

"No problem, sweetie," Dottie answered. "Can we come in?"

"Oh, oh, yeah, please. Stay quiet, though, I have no idea what my father would do if he knew you were here, any of you," she added as she looked at the two of us. "He's just been acting rather strange."

I never wanted to reach out and hold someone in an attempt to make them feel better in my life.

I wasn't exactly that kind of guy.

But with Sybil, suddenly I wanted to.

We entered the home as quietly as we could. Sybil led us through the home and out the back to another small home-like building past the pool.

"Is this where you're staying?" Dottie asked.

Sybil nodded. "It lets me have my own privacy, even though I still have my room inside." Then, after closing the doors, she looked at me. "Who are these guys?" she asked Dottie with a little sidelong glance.

"Uh, this is Jalok and Cazak." Dottie's voice got very precise. "They're Skotans, they're cousins, and they're how I got here so fast."

"Did you have to bring them with you, though?"

Dottie narrowed her eyes. "Well, if something goes really wrong, they can protect us."

"What if they're the cause for what goes wrong? I mean, not to blame you guys," she said with a nod to me. "But, if my dad is suddenly being possessed by whatever is messing with people, won't they actually be a catalyst, or whatever the word is?"

Jalok rolled his eyes and took a seat on a stool in the kitchen of the small home that fit in the backyard of the mayor's house.

I tried my best to smile a nonthreatening, non-creepy smile, but I'm not sure it worked as much as I hoped. She returned my smile, but it seemed more perfunctory than genuine.

As she told Dottie about what had happened, I tried my best to pay attention, but I struggled to do so. I found myself mesmerized by Sybil.

Her skin, with its light brown tones and its supple smoothness, caught my eye and had me daydreaming of being able to touch it, to run my hands across it.

That also made me self-conscious about my own looks. While the loss of my ear and the scar that led to my mouth never truly bothered me, there were a few times where it did make me concerned.

When I was first around the children, I was worried it would scare them. But they were okay with me.

Now, while looking at Sybil and listening to her voice, a voice that sounded beautiful to me, I started to worry about how I looked. I turned my broken side away from her so she wouldn't have to look at it.

Unfortunately, this put me in position to see Jalok better, and he noticed me turning away.

"What are you doing?" he mouthed at me.

After a quick glance at the girls to see if they were looking at me, I mouthed back. "Nothing. Just shifting. Trying to get comfortable."

"Don't lie to me. You like her, don't you?"

"What?" I said, trying to make my face look like he

had said something stupid. "I was trying to get comfortable, that's all."

"Uh-huh." He turned back to the conversation that the girls were having, but every once in a while, he would reach up and mess with his ear. It was his way of showing that he knew why I had turned away from them.

"I promise," Dottie said. "I'll try to help you as best I can."

Jalok's comm rang. "What?" he muttered into it. "Really?"

A pause. "Fine. On our way."

He tilted his head to me. "We've got another call."

Dottie nodded. "It might be for the best, really. If it is a 'possession', then I don't want Sybil's dad getting violent if he sees you. Plus,

it'll let me assess the situation."

Jalok and I agreed to leave her, but only if Dottie kept one of the comms with her, just in case.

She rolled her eyes at the idea, but agreed.

We left the small house, and as Dottie and her friend went inside the main house, I wondered if I ever stood a chance of being anything other than a giant red monster to Sybil.

SYBIL

Once Jalok and his intriguing friend Cazak departed and we returned to the main house, Dottie plopped down onto the loveseat next to me and gave me a warm hug.

I returned her embrace, feeling better already.

Not better enough to return to the living area, however. One look at the area rug or the chandelier brought back memories of my father's strange rage. Dottie and I were sitting in what my father called the den, even though he hardly ever used it.

"Are you feeling any better?" Her voice was muffled because she spoke into my shoulder.

"Yes, I am. Thank you so much for coming over. It really means a lot."

"Hey, we've always been there for each other, ever since elementary school."

We broke apart and she pulled her knees up under her. Dottie'd always been on the petite side, which brought up something I'd been dying to ask her ever since she arrived.

"So, you and Jalok are a thing, right?"

Dottie positively beamed. It wasn't the jittery, anxious look of a woman who was just beginning to date a guy. It was more like the glowing smile of a woman who's met 'the one'.

"Yeah, we're a thing, all right. He might look mean, but he can be so sweet when he wants to."

"And here I thought there wasn't any room in your life for any man other than the Puppet Master."

Dottie laughed, and rocked back and forth on the loveseat.

"Oh, the Puppet Master's not the possessive type. He's more like the ancient organism who barely understands the trivialities of our brief existences."

"That sounds kind of scary."

"Nah." Dottie shook her head. "He's just a big teddy bear, really. At least, he's always been nice to yours truly."

I looked at her through narrowed eyes.

"Well, I think he must have turned you on to non-human guys."

Dottie misinterpreted my expression and tone, and her gaze hardened.

"What's that supposed to mean? Are you going to give me a hard time for dating an alien?"

"What? No!" I put my hands up defensively. "No, nothing like that. I don't mind one way or the other, I really don't. I'm just surprised, that's all."

Dottie relaxed and settled back into her seat.

"Good, because I've gotten enough flak about it from people I work with. I don't understand why some people are so prejudiced against the *Vengeance* crew. Without them, we'd probably all be dead."

"You're probably right." I tilted my head to the side and gave her a sloe-eyed smile. "Still, Jalok seems a lot different from the last guy you dated. What was his name? Tru?"

Dottie squealed and rolled her eyes.

"Oh, that guy. Dru. His name was Dru."

I shook my head sadly.

"You know what I and the rest of our friends were thinking the whole time you were with him?"

"No, what?"

"What in the hell is Dot doing with that peabrained imbecile?"

We laughed in unison, because my description was not far off.

"I kind of figured that." She shook her head and sighed. "He was pretty thickheaded."

"Remember the time he tried to get a Sorvuc drunk by pouring vodka into its venom hole?"

"Yes. He needed like twenty stitches after that."

"God, what a dunderhead. What were you thinking?"

"I was thinking that he had an eight pack and a really big—"

"Dottie!"

"—car. You have to admit he was kind of hot."

I scrunched up my face in concentration, trying to decide if I could ever consider Dru hot.

"I don't know. Sure, he had a nice body, and nice definition in his arms, but he had that look."

I put on a dazed expression, letting my lower lip droop and looking about with an unfocused gaze.

"Uh, hey, baby. You want to blow this place and maybe blow me instead?"

Dottie was overcome with laughter, nearly falling off the loveseat.

"Oh god, he didn't really ever say that."

"Close enough. His innuendo never made it past the sixth grade. You have to admit I got the face right."

"I know you did, but please stop making it, I'm having flashbacks."

Of course, that caused me to gleefully re-adopt my Dru face.

"Hey, darlin', did you fall from heaven? Because if I was in charge of the alphabet, I'd put us together."

"God, stop." Dottie's face had turned red, and tears formed at the corners of her eyes. "I'm going to pee myself if you don't stop."

"Sorry." I shook my head and sighed. I'd really needed Dottie worse than I had thought. "Things have sure been strange lately. I'm so glad you've always had my back."

"Hey, what are friends for?" Dottie spread her hands and grinned. "Didn't I cover for you with the teacher when you snuck out of class for a makeout session with Roy whatshisname?"

"Oh god, don't bring that up. I can still taste the orange soda and cheese puffs on his breath. Besides, it's not like there wasn't reciprocity. I totally covered for you when your mom called my house after you told her you were sleeping over—but were really at an adult party instead."

Dottie sighed and leaned back against the arm of the loveseat. She stretched her legs out over my lap, just as she'd been doing since we were kids.

"It's so good to catch up with you. I've been so busy, it's hard to keep in touch with any of the old gang."

"Yeah, well, between you and me, you aren't missing much."

"What's the matter?"

I described, in detail, the incident with the anti-alien rhetoric the day after the New Year's party, and how I'd stormed away from them all. Dottie seemed somewhat relieved by my story. I think she really had been worried how I was going to take her hooking up with an alien guy.

"Next time, tell those assholes I am going to kick their asses if they don't know when to shut up."

"Small-but-mighty Dottie strikes again."

"Hey, I mean it. I've been through some stuff since the last time we spoke. I nearly got killed in a riot, for one. Of course, that's where I met Jalok, so I guess I shouldn't complain."

"Mmm. I guess you can't deny fate when it comes knocking."

"Guess not. You know what else you can't deny?"

I arched my eyebrow in query.

"What?"

"My rumbling belly. We need some snacks, girl."

"All right, I'll go scrounge something up."

"No, you won't. You're going to sit right there while I take care of you."

I laughed, but when I tried to rise up and help anyway, Dottie knocked me back onto the loveseat with a nifty leg-trip. I wondered if she'd learned it from Jalok. I was too busy laughing to ask at the time.

Dottie wandered into the kitchen, and soon I heard the clink of ceramic platters and the buzzing of the food prep machines. I sighed and relaxed on the loveseat, feeling very warm and loved.

Since I felt as if the crisis with my father was, if not over, at least seeming more distant, I allowed myself to relax a bit and consider Dottie's relationship with the alien, Jalok. I wasn't sure if I'd ever seen her look quite so happy. I guess love really was blind.

Not that Jalok was hard to look at, not at all. But who I had really found intriguing was his companion, Cazak. There was a kind of presence he had, something intangible that I couldn't put into words, that made him seem both intriguing and an enigma.

I bet he was one of those kinds of people who played their cards close to their chest.

He was oddly silent during their visit, but I had noticed him looking at me when he thought I wasn't paying attention.

I didn't know if he was really interested or not, but Cazak was definitely checking me out.

Frankly, the thought thrilled me.

Cazak was certainly nothing like the privileged, spoiled, party boys I normally hooked up with. His eyes seemed both stoic and haunted at the same time, which I supposed came from being a warrior.

But there was a strength of character there in his gaze, something that said he'd already seen hell and refused to be broken. His body certainly wasn't unattractive, that was for certain. The sleek, yet muscled lines of his form were quite pleasing, even beneath the confines of his uniform.

As Dottie puttered about in the kitchen, I found myself wondering what it would be like to be held by those big, powerful arms.

In my mind's eye, I could almost feel his hands caressing my long hair, then sliding down to the small of my back and squeezing me tightly against him.

My fantasies soon took over. I imagined myself nuzzling up to his chest, resting my cheek against the smooth slabs of muscle. More than anything, I recalled his scent. Something akin to peat moss and lilac, but neither of those things.

It wasn't unpleasant, far from it.

"Okay, I got cheese and luurizi and koovar nuts."

I sat up rapidly in the loveseat, shaking my head quickly to blow away those thoughts.

I needed to change my life, sure.

But throwing myself at a Skotan warrior probably wasn't the best way to do it.

No matter how tempting he was.

CAZAK

Once we were back in the aircar, Jalok put the comm on speaker.

"Hey, we have a supply drop heading for Kaster," Sk'lar's voice snapped out. "Inside the shuttle is some new security gear that the mayor requested, all the way from Duvest. You should be there when it arrives."

Jalok and I looked at one another. "When does the shuttle get here?"

"About two hours. Vrehx figured that since you were already there, you could supervise the arrival. The mayor had his own people scheduled to pick it up, but there's some sort of snafu and they can't make it until tomorrow. Vrehx wants to make sure that it's properly unloaded and put away," he answered.

I dropped my head. Not exactly what I'd anticipated

doing with my day, but then, I didn't have a clue what my day was going to be anyway, so this, at least, was something to do. I looked up at Jalok. "What do you say?"

"What can we say? We're essentially under orders," he said.

"Not essentially," Sk'lar cut in over the comm. "Exactly. Vrehx wants you two specifically, mostly because you're already in town. It's tech that we've been helping the engineers at Duvest make, so we're *really* wanting it in the right hands, understand?"

I caught his meaning. "Got it," I said.

"Good. Get your asses over there."

The comm clicked off and Jalok looked at me. "Got what, exactly?"

I loved my cousin, but there were times he wasn't exactly the fastest to pick up on subtle clues.

"We helped make the security gear. And the general wants it secured. It seems pretty clear that if it fell into either the anti-alien faction's hands, or the hands of anyone affiliated with them, then that would be a problem."

"Ah, I understand now. You really think we might have any problems with that?"

"You never know," I said. "Do you want to risk it? Or worse, risk ignoring an order from the general?"

"Well, let's get going then."

We made our way to the airfield, leaving a message for Dottie to let her know where we were going.

On the way to the airfield, we got another comm. "Delivery has been delayed by a couple hours. Try to stay out of trouble," Sk'lar ordered. "And no whining about plans changing."

I shot Jalok a glance. He'd been about to say something, but Sk'lar hung up too quickly.

"Hey," Jalok said after a moment. "While we're in town, I want to go see Adam."

"Um, no," I said back. "You do remember that he's the one that attacked you and tried to kill you, right?"

"Yes," he said in exasperation. "I do remember that. But he wasn't himself, and I'd like to see if he's been able to clean up."

"Really? Seriously?"

"Yes. I know he lost it, but did you know he checked himself back into the facility?" he asked. "He feels better, but decided it wasn't worth the risk of being out in public. Doesn't that sound like someone who's trying to make amends?"

"Or doesn't want to cook for himself," I grumbled.

"I'd like to go," Jalok insisted. "Dottie would like it if we checked in on him."

"What, you need my protection or something?" I asked.

"Kiss off," he said, but he smiled when he said it.

I shrugged. "Fine, let's go. But just so we understand that honesty is key to any relationship, including familial ones, I don't like this idea. I don't think it'll be good, like you're hoping."

"I'm not hoping for anything, just curious," he answered back as he hailed a courier. When inside, he directed the driver to the facility where Adam was being held.

It wasn't hard to get inside; the people there already knew Jalok and knew about his connection to Adam. We were let in quickly.

Adam was given a seat. He seemed calm and collected and even cheerful. But this man had tried to kill Jalok. "Jalok, my friend! How are you?"

"Um, doing well. How are you, Adam?" Jalok answered. I was assuming that Adam's sudden giddiness at seeing the man he'd nearly killed was a shock to my cousin.

"I'm happy to hear that. So, what can I do for you, my friend?"

"Well, why aren't you in restraints?"

"What?" Adam looked genuinely confused for a moment, then his eyes went wide in understanding. "Ah, you hadn't heard. I'm sorry, I tried to have them call you. What you did for me, I want to thank you for that. I also want to apologize for attacking you and trying to kill you. It wasn't something that I'm proud of.

I mean it. So, I hear that you and Dottie are still together? Am I right?"

"I'm not sure if I should..."

"Oh, don't worry about it. If you guys are, I'm happy for you. She deserves to be happy, and if you're the one making her happy, then I'm all for it. I mean it. Look," he said as he sat back and leaned his chair back on two legs, "I know that this is really odd. I get that. You probably came in expecting me to be angry, that I still hate you, that I still spend my nights dreaming up ways to kill you. But," and here he smiled. I'm sure it was a genuine smile, but it bothered me greatly. "I don't. I'm grateful to you. I really am. I'm assuming you took a look at all my brain scans and reports before you walked in, right?"

"We did," Jalok admitted.

We had, too. Adam's brain scans had come back perfect.

No abnormalities, no lesions, nothing at all that would indicate that there was anything wrong with him. In fact, the people that ran the facility said that Adam was a truly changed man and that he was even trying to help people understand that the world had changed and that the crew of the *Vengeance* were trying to make things better.

"So, you can see that I'm fine. No weird things in my scans, no 'possessions' or anything like what I've been hearing about on the news, nothing. I'm honestly happy, and I'm honestly trying to make things better around here. I want to make things right for all of us here."

"Why don't I believe you?" I asked.

Adam looked a little disappointed before he answered me. "Because I did things, said things, thought things, and probably even wrote things down, that were derogatory, inflammatory, and downright asshole-like in regards to you and the rest of your shipmates."

He sighed. "Here's the thing. I'm not perfect. I'm still not fully on the alien-pride parade, I'll admit that. But what I can tell you is that I do understand and accept that you guys are here, that the Xathi weren't your fault, and that you're trying your best to help us all. That's all I can ask, and I'm trying to get people to understand that."

"That sounds positively enlightened," I said. I didn't believe him, not for a second. But I could see that Jalok was buying it.

"That sounds good," he said. "I'm glad to hear that you're doing better. I know Dottie will be happy to hear that."

Adam's face fell a bit. "I feel bad for hurting her, I do. I feel bad for hurting you. There's still something deep inside me that wants me to attack you, I'll admit that to you. But I'm able to hold it back. I'm able to control the feeling, and I'm able to use the feeling to help me talk to others that have a legitimate hatred for you guys. As for my sister, I haven't really talked to her much in the last month. She's only commed once, actually. She doesn't seem too sure about me."

Because you're a possessed homicidal maniac, I thought to myself.

"I'm sorry about that," Jalok said. "If you think it would help, I could try to talk to her."

"Maybe, but I don't want to push her," Adam said. "So, what else did you want to talk about?"

For the next two hours, we sat and talked. Rather, I should say that he and Jalok spoke for two hours and I contributed a few sentences every now and then.

After they were finally finished talking, Adam went back to doing whatever it was that he did inside the facility, and my cousin and I left.

"What was that all about?" I asked.

"What?"

"That whole two hours we just spent in there? You do know he's most likely lying through his teeth, right?"

"Why do you think so?"

"Because the only thing that he was honest about was still having something inside him," I said.

"Why are you so against the idea that he's trying to make things right? Why is it so hard to believe that he's fixing things?" my cousin asked me as he stopped walking, forcing me to stop, as well.

"Really? The man that tried to put a knife into your chest is suddenly being nice?"

"If he was possessed, then it wasn't his fault, and he's maintained the entire time that he wasn't trying to kill me, that he didn't know why he suddenly had that urge," he said. He threw his hands up and gave me a disappointed look. "Why can't you simply accept that?"

"I don't know. I guess, when someone tries to kill my family, it's hard to forgive."

"Well, figure it out." Then he walked off, heading for Sybil's.

"What about Dottie? Any idea why she hasn't said anything to her brother lately?"

"No. But, that's between them. I might bring it up with her, but it's also between her and her brother. Why are you suddenly so concerned about Adam and Dottie now?"

"I'm worried about Dottie, not Adam," I said. "Sorry. Didn't mean to upset you."

"You're fine, just confusing. Speaking of confusing, what was that whole turning away thing back at Sybil's? Since when have you been the type to hide your scar? I mean, your hair covers the lack of the ear, unless you brush it back."

I rolled my eyes and shook my head. "Again, I was

trying to get comfortable. That seat was aggravating my backside."

"Whatever, liar," he laughed.

We changed subjects and went back to cracking stupid jokes as we headed back to the women.

SYBIL

The sound of the front door opening startled both Dottie and me into alertness. We had descended into a cheese-fueled lethargy after our snack binge, but now we were all too alert.

My father came into the parlor, then noticed us sitting in the den. He came walking toward us, completely unhurried and not in the least aggressive. That damned blank expression was still on his face.

"Hi, Dad." I swallowed hard, fearing another outburst, but he remained placid. "How was your day?"

"My day was productive, daughter Sybil." He turned his gaze upon Dottie, but there was neither warmth nor the glimmer of recognition. I waited for him to greet her, but he just continued to stand there and stare blankly.

"Uh, you remember Dottie, don't you? She's only been coming over to our house since, like, forever."

A smile stretched over his face, but it was a cold smile that stayed on his lips and didn't reach his oddly staring eyes.

"Of course I remember Dottie. I remember all of my offspring's friends. Hello, Dottie."

"Hello." Dottie waved weakly, exchanging a wide-eyed glance with me. Both of us definitely felt creeped out. "I understand that you and Sybil had something of a tiff the other night."

"No, we had no tiff. This is a tiff-free home."

I looked to Dottie as if to say *see?* Her gaze remained fixed on my father, however.

"Uh, so you guys didn't get into an argument the other day? Because Sybil seemed pretty upset when I spoke to her about it."

I winced at the note of accusation in Dottie's tone, but my father didn't seem to notice. Or if he did notice, he didn't react in the slightest.

"Oh, yes. That's right. I'm afraid that as a parent I must sometimes lay down the law to my offspring. It's a normal thing that hu—that people do. I'm sure you understand how it was just as painful for me as it was for my daughter Sybil."

"Mr. Anatosian, are you feeling all right?" Dottie cocked her head to the side.

"Why, I feel right as rain, Dottie, right as rain. I'm sure that all of my vital signs are perfectly normal at this time."

He smiled again, but the effect was chilling rather than comforting.

"Well, you seem a little off to me. Maybe you should go see a doctor."

The smile grew just a bit more intense.

"Oh, that won't be necessary. I'm not off. I'm just enacting new disciplinary rules for my offspring. That is a normal thing that happens in society every day. I'm not sure why you think that to be odd."

Dottie sighed in exasperation.

"Maybe I'm just really confused, but you should know that you really upset Sybil with your antics yesterday. Have you even thought about talking to her about how she feels?"

"Ah, you are speaking of that instance." The smile returned to full width, but again, his gaze remained creepy and cold. "Yes, I am afraid that I had to make some hard decisions as the parental unit. Sybil is not allowed to be with anyone I have not vetted properly. I have to make sure they are safe for her to be around. These are dangerous times."

"Yes, but you've never been like this with her before. It's just a sudden change, and we were wondering—"

"Dottie, I appreciate your concern for daughter

Sybil, but my decisions are final. Now if you'll excuse me, I must attend to some business pertaining to my duties as mayor."

Dottie and I exchanged worried, fearful glances. I took her hand and led her upstairs to my room. After securing the door with both a lock and a chair tilted under the doorknob, we sat on my bed and spoke in low tones so he could not hear us downstairs.

"Do you see what I mean? He isn't acting like himself at all."

"There's been nothing overt, but yeah, that's definitely not the Mayor Anatosian that I know." Dottie sighed. "Are you sure you never saw any weird flashes in his eyes?"

"Positive. I'd have definitely noticed something like that. Why are you asking, anyway? Is that a symptom of a disease or something?"

"I didn't notice one either." Dottie held her face in her hands for a moment, and seemed to be struggling with herself. "Sybil, what I'm about to tell you is classified, top-secret military information, but I think you need to hear it. But you can't tell *anyone*, or I could get into a heap of trouble."

"Wait, what?" I shook my head. "Why would you need to tell me classified information? What exactly is going on?"

"There's something I haven't told you. You

remember how I said over comms that I'd found my missing brother, Adam?"

"Yeah, I was really happy for you, and him."

Dottie sighed and seemed on the verge of tears.

"Well, he came back all right, but now he's in the detention center."

"He's what? Oh my god, what happened?"

"He attacked Jalok with a knife, tried to kill him."

"Dottie. No." I shook my head, unable to comprehend what she was saying. "Adam's always been a little hotheaded, but I can't see him becoming violent."

"Me neither. Adam would never do something like that in his right mind. Thing was, he wasn't in his right mind, not at all."

"You're going to have to explain."

"There are these—we don't know what to call them. They're incorporeal beings, that apparently have existed for tens of thousands of years. The Puppet Master calls them the Ancient Enemies, or the old ones."

"Incorporeal?" I struggled with the term. "Does that mean, you can't touch them?"

"Hey, you remember physics class. Yeah, they don't have what we would call physical forms. They seem to exist as pure conscious energy, as mystifying as that sounds. Anyway, since they don't have physical bodies, we suspect they've learned to take them over from other species, like humans."

I stared at her in complete shock, my mouth hanging open.

"Take them over? Like demonic possession?"

"Yes, only for real. And it's not always obvious when it happens, but every other time the phenomenon has been reported, there's been a strange flash of light in the affected human's eyes. They sweat a lot, too."

"My dad was sweating the other day."

"Yes, but he was really worked up. In science, we have a saying that goes like this, 'Sometimes a unicorn is just a horse.'"

"Sometimes a unicorn is just a horse? What the hell does that even mean?"

Dottie chuckled softly, though she didn't have the heart for much mirth.

"I suppose it is a strange expression. What it means is, just because you encounter unknown phenomena doesn't mean that there's not a sound, logical explanation for it. So, if you found hoofprints in the forest, you could claim they were from a unicorn, but the fact is, it was probably a horse."

It took me a moment to piece together what she'd said.

"So, just because my dad was sweating profusely, it doesn't necessarily mean he's been possessed?"

"Right. And most of those people who have been possessed were only under the control of the Ancient Enemies for a short time. So it's possible your father is just succumbing to the stress of his job and being a single parent."

"This is horrifying." I hugged myself and shivered, though it wasn't cold in my upstairs bedroom. "How far has this reached?"

"Pretty far. They say that one of the candidates was possessed during the debates a while back."

"Is that what happened?" Of course, I hadn't watched the debates---there was a sick party going on that night—but I'd heard about the violence which erupted later.

"Yeah. And it happened to Adam, too."

"Is Adam going to be all right?"

"Near as we can tell, he is. They have him in detention for observation, but he's shown no further signs of possession."

Dottie grimaced and stared out the window.

"It's hard to pin down how widespread it is, because there's plenty of legitimate anti-alien sentiment to go around. The anti-alien terrorists cause plenty of havoc all on their own without any help from ancient, incorporeal beings."

"This is just too much. I don't think I can even handle this, Dottie. I kind of wish you hadn't told me."

"I know. I know it's a burden, but I thought you should know, in case—in case your dad is—"

"In case we really are dealing with a unicorn, and not a horse."

Dottie spread her hands as if to say that I'd gotten the gist of what she wanted to say. I guess it was hard for her to come out and say the words 'if your father has been possessed'.

If I hadn't been in turmoil before, I certainly was now. My father's strange behavior paled in comparison to the idea that there were malevolent forces plotting our doom. Forces which could not be seen, or touched, or sensed in any way except by the effect they had on their hosts.

"So," I started, stopped again. This wasn't a sentence I'd ever thought I'd say. "How do we tell if my father is possessed?"

Dottie reached for her comms unit. "I can think of one thing, but you might not like it."

As she made her call, my mind raced.

Was my father just feeling the strain of his high-powered position and my admittedly exasperating behavior?

Or was he really under the control of the Ancient Enemies?

Somehow, not knowing was the worst part of it all.

CAZAK

The sun had sunk low on the horizon, casting a golden-red glow on Jalok and me as we finally lugged the mayor's deliveries to his office.

"They say it's too sensitive to trust to anyone but a *Vengeance* crewmember, but I think the government really just wanted to avoid paying delivery fees," Jalok muttered.

"Regardless, it's nearly done," I said.

Mayor Anatosian, like most prideful humans, had set up his office on the top floor of the Kaster municipal building. Jalok and I rode the elevator up to the top in silence, as I was lost in thought and he was all gooey-eyed over the prospect of seeing his sweetheart, Dottie.

No matter how I tried to think about something

else, my mind kept dwelling on Mayor Anatosian's daughter, Sybil. I never thought I would be part of the 'attracted to human women' club, not in a million years. Because of that, I hadn't figured my scar for being an issue.

Skotans see scars as a sign of strength, like a big flashing sign that says, 'look what I've survived'. But humanity was different. They praised youth and beauty in their literature, poetry, and artwork.

I found myself avoiding looking at my reflection in the elevator car's polished metal walls on the ride up. After years of learning to live with my disfigurement, it was suddenly making me self-conscious.

All because of the mayor's daughter. I tried not to think about her sweetly curved body, or her long silken hair, because by default, she was out of my league.

We got to the top floor and hauled our burdens to the reception area. The bright-eyed young woman behind the desk smiled at Jalok, but her grin became strained when her gaze fell on me. I turned my head to the side so as to hide my ugliness.

"Hello. We have some packages for Mayor Anatosian."

"Oh, I'm sorry, but I'm afraid the mayor isn't in right at the moment."

Jalok's eyes narrowed in annoyance and he kicked one of the boxes.

"Then what are we supposed to do with these? Drag them back outside?"

"No, you can leave those with me and I'll see to it the mayor gets them."

"As long as you can sign that you received it and we can verify that they're secure."

"The mayor has a secure office for deliveries," she responded. "He and I are the only ones coded for access."

"Very well," Jalok growled after checking with Sk'lar.

Jalok signed over the delivery to the receptionist and we turned to leave. At the last moment, I caught the woman staring at my face out of the corner of her eye. No doubt my appearance horrified her, but I did my best to ignore her reaction.

On the way back down to the main floor, Dottie called. "Can you guys come back? Nothing's wrong, I just want to test a theory."

Jalok was beside himself with anticipation. Since our duty had been discharged, he now had the opportunity to spend some time with his girlfriend and see what she had uncovered.

My wager was, this whole trip was just another false alarm, dreamed up as a transformation during a domestic dispute between father and daughter.

But going back to check on things meant that I

would be likely to run into Sybil again, and be tormented again by things that I could never have.

My mind raced with different ideas. I came up with and rejected several excuses not to go with Jalok. Then I tried to convince myself that Sybil probably wouldn't even be home, instead would be out enjoying the life of a young socialite.

Naturally, I knew that my hopes were likely in vain, but it was all I could do to keep my anxiety in check. On the way to the mayor's house, I also spent time trying to figure out a way to cover up my disfigurement.

I came up with the idea of always keeping my head turned away from her, but quickly rejected that notion. All I would have done was make it obvious I was trying to hide the scar.

As we strolled down the avenue, Jalok going on and on about something I didn't care to discuss, I stopped at a shop selling hats. Jalok continued on up the street, still running his mouth, until he realized I was no longer abreast of him.

He returned to the shop just as I was trying on a wide brimmed straw hat. Unfortunately, it didn't do much to hide my face. I was just considering trying on a scarf when Jalok burst out laughing.

"What the fuck are you doing?"

"Just trying on a hat, what's the big deal?"

"You've never even looked at hats before. What gives? Are you embarrassed to be seen with me because I'm dating a human girl?"

"Get over yourself for a nanosecond. I'm a feared Skotan warrior and I'll try on hats if I want to, with or without your approval."

I stalked out to the street in anger, leaving Jalok in my wake. He tried several times to engage me in conversation the rest of the way to Dottie but I didn't give him the satisfaction.

The mayor's house was a nicely appointed home with landscaping and those running lights by the sidewalk rich folks seemed to enjoy. The whole way up the walk, I felt like a condemned man walking to his execution.

There was no way to hide my disfigurement from Sybil. Surely, she would find my scarred visage hideous and nauseating, but there was nothing I could do.

We were shown into the home and led to a parlor, where Dottie and Sybil sat with beverages, going over the information from Nyheim.

Jalok and Dottie briefly kissed, and I stayed around behind him, hoping I would escape notice.

Sybil's gorgeous face turned my way, and she actually smiled. I could detect no trace of any disgust in her expression, but being a politician's child, she was probably skilled at hiding her true feelings behind a staged smile. I couldn't take the scrutiny and turned away, staring out the window at the fading sunlight.

"So, what's your theory, beautiful?" Jalok wrapped his arms around Dottie and dropped a kiss on the top of her head.

"Let's just stay here for a while and see what happens, alright?" Dottie shrugged. "I don't want to influence the results by telling you too much."

Sybil rolled her eyes. "You've been using that line since school. Sometimes you have to tell people actual facts, you know?"

Dottie and Jalok chatted, mostly about what she'd been working on. Sybil's musical laughter joined in with their own, and I felt more alone, more isolated and unwanted, than I ever had in my life.

As the three of them chitchatted, I tried to pretend I was interested in some of the books lining the walls, but I couldn't even register what language they were in.

The sound of the door opening heralded the arrival of Mayor Anatosian himself.

Watching the tenseness in Sybil's shoulders, I could guess what Dottie's theory was. I hoped for everyone's sake she was wrong.

The august personage smiled when he saw his daughter. I'd seen him before, but not this close. He was a relatively unimpressive-looking human, not rippled with muscle like some I'd seen, but possessed of a certain presence that probably served him well in politics.

"Hi, Daddy." Sybil smiled sweetly at her father. She gestured to Cazak and me, the movement only slightly stiff. "Have you met my friends, Jalok and Cazak?"

Anatosian's gaze snapped over to Jalok, then to me. A strange flash of light came over his eyes, and I instantly became alert. Wasn't that supposed to be a sign of the Ancient Enemies trying to possess someone's mind?

"What is the meaning of this?" Anatosian's face turned red as the fading sun, and his nostrils flared out with each labored breath. His hands clenched and unclenched into fists at his sides.

"Daddy, what's wrong? Why are you—"

"I don't want—alien scum—my house—kill you."

"What?"

Anatosian's eyes narrowed to slits and a guttural growl escaped his throat. Suddenly he wasn't moving like a middle-aged human, but more like a predatory animal. Veins stood out on his forehead and arms as he worked himself into a lather, snarling and snapping like a beast.

"Daddy, what are you doing?"

With a howl of rage, the mayor of Kaster launched himself right at Jalok. If it had been me, I would have tried to restrain the mayor without hurting him, but

Jalok was Jalok. So my cousin reached out and snapped a right cross against the mayor's jaw.

Jalok and I were from a high-gravity world. A mere tap from either of us should have been enough to lay out even a burly human, let alone a middle-aged pencil pusher.

Instead, Anatosian didn't even flinch. His grasping hands sought out Jalok's vulnerable eyes even as my cousin summoned his scaled armor to the forefront.

"Cazak, don't just stand there, help me!"

The note of desperation in Jalok's tone made me leap into action. My final thought as I summoned my own scales was that now my face would look even worse, twisted up with anger and exertion. I probably looked like a monster to Sybil.

I came up behind Mayor Anatosian and grabbed him around the chest. I attempted to pull him off Jalok, but his grip was much stronger than I'd anticipated.

The three of us bounced around off the walls and smashed through a low coffee table in our struggle. Despite there being two of us, Mayor Anatosian was proving to be a daunting challenger.

Of course, I should point out that the two of us were striving not to hurt him badly, whereas he was vicious, an animal on the attack.

With effort, I managed to pry his hands away from Jalok's throat, but then he turned his attention to me.

Then the bastard bit me. Actually fucking bit me! Civilian security came pouring through the door, but stopped dead in their tracks to take in the spectacle of an elected official sinking his teeth into a Skotan.

I wasn't about to smash Sybil's father's brains in right in front of her. His strength was nearly equal to my own, but I managed to keep him at bay long enough for Jalok to sneak up behind him.

Jalok wrapped his arms around the good mayor's neck in a sleeper hold, cutting off the flow of blood to his brain. Soon Anatosian slumped in my cousin's grip, limbs going slack.

"Do you think it was—" Jalok's voice trailed off, because he didn't want to spill classified information in front of civvies.

"Had to be. Let's take him back to a facility ourselves."

The civilian security team didn't argue the point as I called in a shuttle to ferry Mayor Anatosian away in.

I couldn't help but think that Sybil must have been truly horrified with me, not just for being ugly, but for beating up her father in her own home.

She couldn't be more disgusted with my actions than I was.

SYBIL

A hovercar with the official seal of the Nyheim-Allied Worlds League pulled up in front of my home. When Dottie said she had arranged for a ride to take me to the airport, I didn't think she meant this. The driver was a stern-looking K'ver.

I stood at the rear passenger door and stared at my reflection. When it became obvious that the driver wasn't going to get out and let me in, I pulled the door open myself. I felt numb as I plopped myself in the seat. I threw my bag on the seat in front of me. I don't even remember packing.

"Where are we going?" I asked the driver.

"There's an aerial unit heading to a site near Nyheim. You're catching a ride with them."

"Oh."

Great.

We drove in silence. I had a million questions I wanted to ask, but the driver didn't seem like much of a talker. The odds that he had the answers to my questions were slim to none, anyway.

"Do you know if a human named Dottie will be there?" I asked.

"Don't know," came the curt reply. Obviously, this wasn't the job the K'ver had signed up for. I wondered if he was being punished or something.

It wasn't until the car came to a stop that I realized we weren't taking a flight out of the regular airport. We drove through a military base milling with aliens and humans alike. The driver followed directions to an airstrip crudely carved out of the ground. He came to a stop, turned the hovercar off, and then just sat there.

"What next?" I asked after a few moments.

"You get out."

"I'm going through a fucking traumatic experience over here. Would it kill you to be a little nicer?"

"Have a nice day, ma'am," he tossed over his shoulder. I grabbed my bag and jumped out of the car.

Dottie found me at once. Cazak was with her. He had a white gauze patch taped over where Dad had bitten him. I couldn't keep my eyes from the wound. My father had done that.

My father!

"How is it?" I asked him.

He didn't look at me or speak. Instead, he gave a shrug and walked off toward the aerial unit I guessed we were taking.

"I still don't understand what's happening," I told Dottie.

"Your father's being transferred with us to a detention facility."

I felt the blood drain from my face.

"I know it sounds scary." Dottie placed a hand on my arm. "I've seen the place for myself. It's quite comfortable."

"It's still basically a jail." I bit my bottom lip as tears welled up in my eyes.

"No, it's not," Dottie assured me. "It's more like a hospital. It's comfortable."

"Hospitals aren't comfortable."

I felt bad for shooting down everything Dottie told me. She was just trying to make it easier on me.

Dottie led me to a security checkpoint. My bag was searched for weapons. Turns out, I packed way too many pairs of pants, one jacket, and a cocktail dress, for some reason. I must've been super out-of-it while packing.

"You can borrow whatever you need," Dottie murmured as I watched my belongings get shoved back into my bag.

Next, two Valorni scanned my body from top to bottom. I didn't know what they were looking for, but apparently everything I wore was unacceptable for military air travel. Had I known I was going to be getting on an aircraft today, I wouldn't have worn so much jewelry.

It took ten minutes before I was allowed to board the flight. I'd never been on a public aircraft before. When Dad traveled for work, an aircar was provided for us.

I liked traveling that way. Watching the countryside change was one of my favorite parts of driving. That, and stopping at any place that looked interesting for food or shopping.

I expected seats on the aircraft. Instead, it was just a series of metal benches with straps that went over the chest and shoulders. Dottie took the seat nearest to the body of the plane. There were no windows. I sat next to her. Cazak sat down beside me.

And my father's gurney was fastened to hooks in the floor so it couldn't roll.

I looked away, struggling with the cross straps. They kept getting tangled or bunching all to one side.

Without a word, Cazak reached over and tugged on one of my straps. The harnessed snapped into place so that I could clip myself in.

"Thanks," I said.

Cazak nodded and fixed his gaze straight ahead. Rather than force him into conversation, I turned to Dottie.

"I need you to tell me more," I said.

"I can't tell you much until he's examined. That's not my area of expertise," she replied, her eyes filled with concern.

"Just tell me something. Anything. Even your best guess, I don't care." I knew I sounded crazy but I didn't care. More aliens filed on to the plane and clipped themselves into their seats.

"If it's not the you-know-what," she looked around, and I realized she probably hadn't been supposed to tell me about the people being possessed, "my guess is it's some kind of neurovirus," she said. "He's behaving similar to how Xathi hybrids behaved, only there's no crystallization of the skin."

"But all the Xathi are gone." I turned to Cazak. "Right?"

He gave a curt nod in response.

"That's why we don't know for sure what it is," Dottie continued. "For as many similarities as there are to Xathi hybridism, there are as many differences. We call them 'the possessed'. It's a mystery."

"That's not very comforting." I chewed my bottom lip.

"I'd rather give you honest answers than comfortable ones."

"You're right," I sighed. "I'm sorry. I think I'm still in shock."

"That's only natural." Dottie patted my knee. "Just know that he'll be in the best place he could possibly be. The scientists that cured hybridism will be working with him."

"That helps," I nodded.

"Good. I'm going to try to get one of them in a conference chat." Dottie pulled out a datapad and started tapping away. I decided to let her work. She'd already told me everything she could.

The aircraft took off with a thunderous roar. I clutched my shoulder straps until my knuckles went white. When the aircraft tipped, my stomach felt like it was going to jump into my throat. I squeezed my eyes shut and tried to pretend I was somewhere else, anywhere else.

It took twenty minutes for the aircraft to level out. Only then did I open my eyes. To my surprise, Cazak was staring at me, his expression blank. I wanted to say something, but I couldn't think of anything.

"Thank you," I ended up stammering.

"What?"

"Thank you for not hurting my dad," I said. "He took a good chunk out of you with that bite. You would've been in the right to do some damage in return, but you didn't."

If Cazak was surprised by my words, he didn't show it. He stared at me for a long while before answering.

"You're welcome."

He looked away, fixing his gaze on a point at the far end of the plane.

I noticed he angled his head in a strange way. From where I sat, I couldn't see his scar at all. I wondered if he was doing that on purpose.

Was he ashamed of his scar? That seemed silly. He was a giant, powerful, dedicated soldier. It seemed only natural that he would acquire some scars along the way. As strange as it was, I liked the way his scar looked.

Cazak was handsome, more handsome than any of the human men I took up with out of boredom. There was no point in denying that. He was the first person I'd felt an honest attraction to in the longest time. His scar only added to that.

I wanted to tell him as much, but he didn't seem interested in talking to me. Besides, I didn't know if he found me as attractive as I found him. What if I told him what I thought and he looked at me like I was crazy? What if he wasn't attracted to humans at all?

Dottie and Jalok seemed to be in love, not just in love, but perfectly matched, almost as if it were fated.

That didn't mean every alien was keen on humans as romantic partners.

Why did I care so much? I barely knew Cazak. The thing was, I wanted to know him. He had that quiet, mysterious thing going for him. It was undeniably attractive. Plus, I couldn't shake this feeling that there was so much more to him beneath the gruff exterior. I wanted to know him.

But now didn't exactly seem like the best time to try to get to know him. If I did, it would be more about finding a way not to think about my father than actually listening to what Cazak had to say. Besides, he didn't look like he was in a conversational mood.

I didn't want to annoy him before I had a chance to get to know him better.

I wished the aircraft had windows. I was starting to feel claustrophobic. I looked over at Dottie's datapad. She was frantically typing back and forth with someone, hopefully someone who knew what was happening to my Dad.

"Any news?" I asked before I could stop myself.

"They're going through his readings now," she explained. "Once we actually get him to the facility, they'll be able to do more." She bit her lip. "But you have to understand. The tests are being designed as subjects become available. We just don't have much to work with."

"So, basically, the top scientists are forced to guess?"

"Yes, but they're much better at guessing than anyone else," Dottie smiled. I appreciated that she was trying to make me laugh, but I didn't feel like laughing right now.

"Try not to worry too much," she said. "I know that's the most unhelpful thing to say, but-"

"I know what you mean." I offered her a weak smile. Unfortunately, all I could do was worry.

CAZAK

Our shuttle lurched as it encountered turbulence in the skies over Nyheim.

I had spent most of the flight trying to keep the scarred side of my face turned away from Sybil. There had been a tiny smidge of hope in me that she really didn't mind, but the other voices in my head drowned it out. I still believed that there was no way someone like Sybil could ever be interested in someone like me, not even out of pity.

I glanced over at her out of the corner of my eye and found her speaking to Dottie again. Sybil's lovely face was marred with a worried frown, and she held her unconscious father's hand. It had to bother her that his wrists were strapped to the gurney, but precautions had to be taken.

There was still a lot we didn't know about the Ancient Enemies and any effects they might have had on human physiology. For all we knew, the sedatives would be ineffectual on someone in the throes of possession.

The shuttle settled onto its landing pylons and the back door cracked open, greeting us with an icy blast of wind. Jalok and I each took a side of the gurney and wheeled the mayor down the ramp onto the tarmac.

Sybil took off her own coat and tossed it over Mayor Anatosian's slumbering form. It had been much warmer down on the coast in Kaster.

From the tarmac, we transitioned to an emergency vehicle and transported the good mayor to the detention center. Sybil sniffled and cried when she saw?

the imposing building looming before us, but Dottie attempted to calm her down.

Part of me wished I had the ability, or the right, to do the comforting myself.

Something drew me to her. Not just her beauty, although that was undeniable. Something within her, a spark, that called to me. But I had no right to answer it.

Dottie and Sybil were forced to wait in the lobby while Jalok and I wheeled Mayor Anatosian into the detention center's processing area.

Evie was there and we notified her of the situation.

Grimly, she took charge of our prisoner/patient and directed us to report to General Rouhr directly, rather than using comms. Under the circumstances, given the sensitivity of our charge, I understood completely.

Even as I was forced to leave Sybil behind, I felt conflicted.

On the one hand, I was no longer so self-conscious of my scar without her there. But then I also felt disappointment, as well as relief. I'd barely known Sybil for a day, and already my world felt empty without her presence.

My gut was flipping the whole way to General Rouhr's office. Thoughts of Sybil kept leaping, unbidden, into my mind, but they weren't wholly unpleasant.

But every little fantasy I had didn't end with a mutual declaration of affection, but with her vomiting at the thought of touching my scarred skin.

We were shown into the general's office. The big, aging man glared at us, but he did that with everyone regardless of his mood, or any wrongdoing on their part.

"Cazak. Jalok." He pointed at a pair of seats in front of his desk. "I already read a preliminary report, but I want to hear what happened in your own words."

Jalok and I looked at each other, and he shrugged. Sighing, I went into my report.

"Mayor Anatosian just attacked us, sir. Well, he attacked Jalok first, but then—"

"Then he bit Cazak."

"Bit him?"

General Rouhr turned his gaze onto me.

"Is this true, Cazak?"

"Yes, sir. The mayor wasn't acting like himself, not at all. He was more like, like, an animal."

"Or one of the possessed."

Jalok's words hung in the air, leaving us to exchange worried glances.

"And the two of you did nothing to incite him?" General Rouhr glanced between the two of us, and then for some reason his gaze settled on me. "Nothing at all?"

Why would the general think that I'd done anything? Unlike that hothead, Jalok, I'm pretty laid back. Well, laid back for a Skotan soldier.

General Rouhr stood up and straightened his uniform. Suddenly he seemed old, ancient even. He walked to the window and stared out at the evening sky as a shuttle flew by across the air currents.

"This is the nineteenth case of possession to come across my desk in the last two weeks."

Jalok and I stared in shocked silence. Nineteen? How much did it take before it was considered an epidemic?

"Nineteen, sir?"

Rouhr grunted in response to Jalok's query.

"Nineteen. All of them just as you described. They attacked without warning. The only sign anyone has reported is that they talk differently than normal, but not so much as to be something overt they can be called out on."

"Does it usually involve anti-alien hate-speech?"

"Sometimes. But when it does, it's almost always from someone who is not known for that type of opinion."

"So, the Ancient Enemies are able to twist anyone's mind. They don't need to rely on existing prejudices."

Rouhr cocked an eyebrow at my statement.

"Indeed. That's a remarkable piece of insight, Cazak. Maybe it's time you were promoted to officer."

That idea sent ice shooting through my veins. The thought of being responsible for the whole team was not one that I found appealing.

"I—I'm just a soldier, general. Nothing more, and nothing less."

"That's just what an excellent officer would say, Cazak, but I'll let the matter drop. For now."

I made a mental note to myself to appear more incompetent around the general in the future. Perhaps I should act more like Jalok.

"Sir, what are we going to do?" We both turned to

Jalok, who had an uncharacteristic expression of worry on his orange face. "If the Ancient Enemies can just take over who they please, how can we fight them? What if they're possessing people in this very building right as we speak?"

"What would you have me do, Jalok? Start rounding people up at random and hold them in case they might be possessed?"

Jalok opened his mouth, and then closed it.

"I don't know, sir. Maybe not everyone. Maybe just, just the people who—"

"The people who what, cousin, have been talking skrell about aliens?" I shook my head at his ignorance. "Don't you see what a disaster that would be for us, politically? You might as well hand the anti-alienists a talking point on a silver platter."

Rouhr rubbed his chin and stared at me. I silently cursed myself for appearing smart in front of him. I didn't want to do paperwork.

"Yeah, I guess you're right." Jalok sighed. "I just feel so damn frustrated. How do we fight an enemy we can't even see?"

"With heart, determination, and skill." General Rouhr put his hands behind his back and glared at each of us in turn. "We've faced daunting foes before. The Xathi. The flora and fauna of this planet. Anti-alien extremists. We're professionals. We'll defeat this challenge, too. Dismissed."

Jalok and I left the general's office, then we parted ways. Jalok wanted to go find his girlfriend, of course.

Me, I was still bothered by a lot of things. So, I did what any self-respecting soldier does when circumstances are confusing or beyond our control.

I hit the local tavern.

There were a few guys I knew in there, loitering about, but they took one look at my black expression and left me alone. I drank in silence and solitude, but even though my body was still, my mind raced around in circles.

But I wasn't thinking so much as brooding. If I'd been thinking, I'd have been trying to deal with the Ancient Enemies, finding a countermeasure to their possession.

Instead, I sat and drank while pining for Sybil.

But I kept dwelling on the way she smiled at me. Sure, she smiled at my cousin Jalok, too, but her eyes didn't light up the same way as they did when she turned it to me.

I tried to tell myself that it was because she felt sorry for me. Or maybe she was just being magnanimous toward the guy with the scars, so she felt better about herself.

The one possibility I was afraid to consider was also the one I most fervently hoped was true.

Maybe she really didn't care about my scars. Maybe she was even interested in me the way I was interested in her.

Then I caught my reflection in a chrome lighting fixture, saw the scarred and twisted face and the missing ear, and sunk deeper into depression.

How could someone as beautiful as Sybil be with someone as ugly as me?

SYBIL

I expected the detention center to look like the kind of evil dungeon that always popped up in old Earth fairy tales. Those dark buildings with gargoyles and moats, that always had storm clouds and lightning looming behind them.

Instead, it was just a normal building. I wouldn't go as far as to call it nice. None of the buildings in Nyheim were nice anymore, at least not on the outside.

The Xathi invasion did a number on the city, as did the Puppet Master before he became a friend of the people.

The detention center was located on the outer edge of the town. That made sense. In the event of an escape or some kind of biological contamination, it wouldn't spread to the public right away. There was an electrified fence around the property, but it didn't look like a prison.

From the outside, I could see an exercise yard. I wondered if they'd let my dad outside, since I was there. I hoped so. He didn't like being inside for long periods. Which was ironic, since his job was mostly done from inside an office with only one window.

Dottie came with me, as I figured I wouldn't be able to get past security by myself. I needed her credentials.

"If they question you, just pull rank," she advised me as we entered the building.

"Pull rank?"

"Tell them who your father is. Threaten to get Vidia involved. You pull rank all the time in clubs and restaurants."

"Yeah, but that's for a free appetizer, not to get into a secure facility," I countered. "Besides, I'm off my game. I won't be convincing."

"You don't need to put on an act. You just need to be the concerned daughter you are."

"Whatever you say."

Dottie and I approached the receptionist's desk. I found it funny that a place like this had a receptionist in the first place.

Dottie handed the receptionist her ID card and explained what we were here to do. I had a hard time focusing on the conversation. All I could look at was the security guards and the huge blasters strapped to their waists.

"Visiting hours only apply to approved patients who can receive approved visitors. The patient in question has not been approved yet, so there's nothing I can do," the receptionist told Dottie. She at least had the decency to pretend to look sorry.

Dottie gave me a look then jerked her head toward the receptionist. I was supposed to pull rank now. I took a deep breath and squared my shoulders.

I'd done this a million times before, sometimes just for fun. I knew that made me kind of a shitty person, but perhaps all those times were training me for this moment.

Like cosmic preparation or something.

"My name is Sybil Anatosian." My voice came out trembly and weak. "I want to see my dad." Instead of sounding like a confident, determined woman, I sounded like a scared little girl. Tears welled up in my eyes. I blinked them away.

"Oh, honey," the receptionist hummed. I was so upset that I didn't care how condescending she sounded. "I know you do. If he was on the approved list, I'd let you in during visiting hours. He's not approved just yet. It would be dangerous for me to let you see him. I can put you on the contact list so you know the minute he's approved. That list isn't for civilians. Would that be okay?"

Actually, yes. That would be fine.

"Sure." I nodded and gave her my information. As I was entering my contact info into her datapad, a woman with golden hair strode out into the lobby from the area where the patients were kept.

"Evie?" Dottie perked up. The woman's face split into a wide smile that looked like sunshine.

"Hey, Dottie!" The woman, Evie, walked up to Dottie and gave her a big hug. "I didn't know you were coming in today."

"It wasn't planned. My friend's father was admitted earlier today. We're just trying to get some information."

Evie turned to me with sympathy filled eyes.

"The mayor is your father?" she asked me.

"Yes, ma'am, I'm Sybil."

"I'm so sorry." She reached forward and gave my arm a gentle squeeze. Normally, I wasn't crazy about people I didn't know touching me. However, her touch felt nice, almost motherly. "I'm Dr. Evie Parr. I'm one of the doctors who will be running tests on him later today."

"I thought the testing had already started," I frowned.

"No, he's only just completed his inpatient

examinations. He had to be heavily sedated again," she added quietly.

"How is he now?" I asked.

"Still asleep. We're giving him some time to recover before we start testing. It can be a draining process. We like to make it as smooth and painless as we can for our patients."

"How many are in here?"

"Over two dozen."

"Do they all have the same thing my father has?"

"From what we can tell, yes," she nodded. "What they all have is still a mystery."

"Is it like the hybridism the Xathi unleashed? People changed then, horribly." I remembered all too well. Not even my near-constant partying since the Xathi had been defeated could erase that memory.

Evie's face went ashen but she didn't drop her smile.

"That's one theory. We call them possessed, rather than hybrids, since their physical bodies don't seem to change."

"Evie was part of the team that developed the cure for hybridism," Dottie spoke up.

"Really?" I perked up. "How did you do that? Do you think you can do it again?"

"I'm going to try," Evie laughed nervously.

"I'm sorry. I don't mean to put that kind of pressure

on you. I'm sure you're getting plenty of that from everyone else, too," I said.

"It's okay." Evie smiled kindly. "I have more experience than most with the effects of hybridism. It's only natural that people look to me to fix it."

"What do you mean?" I asked.

Evie pressed her lips together, pondering her words.

"If you don't want to share, you don't have to," I said quickly.

"I think it might give you some peace of mind to know why I'm as qualified as I am. But we shouldn't talk about it here. Step into my office?"

Evie swiped her ID card to open the door to the back rooms. Dottie and I followed.

"You have a permanent office here now?" Dottie asked.

"Sort of. It's also a storage room. Space is cramped around here, but it's okay. I don't need much room. It's not as if my proper office is far away, either."

The room Evie took us to really was a storage room. It was packed to the brim with boxes, with just enough room for a desk and a filing cabinet.

"I hope the labs aren't like this." Dottie looked around the room and wrinkled her nose.

"The labs are pretty nice," Evie replied. "Not as nice as the one in the main building, but a close second."

"That's a relief. Bad equipment can be as detrimental as bad research," Dottie said.

"That won't be a problem here," Evie grinned. "Now, about my little story."

"Right," I nodded. "Go on."

"I don't know how much you know about the Xathi," she began, "but they are a hive-mind species. Their minds are linked to sub-queens. Those sub-queens report back to and take orders directly from the queen of their hive. Hybridism stems from the queens and is inflicted through the sub-queens. Does that make sense?"

I nodded.

"I was working in a clinic in another city studying the first cases of hybridism. Apparently, the queen didn't like that. This was before the aliens set up their base in Nyheim. I was reporting back to their original ship, the *Vengeance,* when the Xathi queen herself attacked my mind."

"That must've been horrible." I chewed my bottom lip.

"It was," Evie nodded. "She somehow accessed my deepest childhood memories and used those against me. It took me a while to break free from her grasp."

"How did you do it?" I asked. A wistful expression passed over Evie's face.

"I heard the voice of someone I loved. It was strong

enough to puncture the shield the Xathi queen set up around my mind. From there, I was able to pull myself out of my memories and fight her off. I wasn't right for several weeks after that."

"I can imagine."

"The Puppet Master has explained what he knows about the Ancient Enemies, but it doesn't give us any way to fight them, much less cast them out of one of their victims." She leaned back against the wall. "Understanding how the Xathi queen took over her slaves helped me figure out how to reverse the damage she did," Evie explained. "I'm hoping the same principles apply to what's happening now."

"I hope so, too." I nervously tugged at a strand of hair. "Is there anything I can do to help? I'll be here in Nyheim until my father's well enough to take home."

If he's ever well enough, that was, but I didn't say it out loud.

"Hearing a familiar voice helped me. Once your father's cleared for visitors, maybe it will help him," Evie suggested. "Until then, I just need you to be patient and put some trust in me. I understand if you can't put all of it, but at least give me some."

"I can do that." For the first time since this nightmare started, I smiled. "Can you do me one favor, though?"

"I can try," Evie shrugged.

"Can you keep me updated?" I asked. "I hate being in the dark about things like this."

"Of course." Evie reached forward to grab my hand. "Anything for a friend of Dottie's."

Relief washed over me.

"Thank you," I sighed. "My dad's the only family I have left. If I lose him-"

I couldn't finish the sentence. Just the thought of it made my throat grow thick.

"We're going to do everything we can to help him," Evie assured me.

Evie walked Dottie and me back to the lobby. I gave them a moment to chat before we left, thinking over everything that had been said.

And everything that hadn't been.

Finally, I decided that if anyone was going to be in charge of my dad's health, I was glad it was Dr. Evie Parr.

She was a fighter. She'd fight for him. And so would I.

CAZAK

Using the barrel of my assault rifle, I gently lifted a thin branch out of my path of vision. The sun didn't penetrate well past the dense foliage of the Nyheim jungle, making the forest floor dark and murky.

When I saw that the clearing ahead was empty, I moved out of my cover and proceeded with great caution, eyes and ears—okay, ear—strained for any sign that I was not alone.

The only problem was, in the jungle you're never alone. Supposedly, our deal with the Puppet Master meant that we were off-limits to the local flora and fauna, but with the Ancient Enemies raising their ugly, incorporeal heads, it didn't hurt to be cautious.

I kept expecting to run into one of the newly possessed at each and every turn of my path, but so far that day, boredom had been my main adversary. Constantly being on high alert can really take it out of you, even if it hadn't been freezing cold.

My mind kept drifting back to Sybil and her father, Mayor Anatosian. It had to be hard for Sybil to have seen her father act like a savage animal. I wanted to be sympathetic to both of them, but the mayor had bitten me.

Of course, on a logical level, I realized that it wasn't his fault. The Ancient Enemies had possessed him, taken control of his body like a marionette.

My feelings for Sybil complicated the matter even further. Seeing me brawl with her father and ultimately drag him away in restraints had to put a crimp in any potential relationship.

Maybe that's why I hadn't complained about being sent out on patrol all by my lonesome in the jungle. I didn't feel very chatty at the time, and if Jalok had been along for the trip, he probably would have been going on and on about Dottie this, Dottie that.

Such musings only served to underscore the fact that I was feeling quite alone and miserable that day.

Sybil kept coming back into my mind, resisting all attempts to banish her. I would see a shadow move in the jungle as the wind stirred stray branches, and it would appear to me as her glorious dark mane of hair.

Or I would see the delicate legs of a hunting avian and it would remind me of her tapered lower limbs. Truly, Sybil was the loveliest member of the human species I had ever seen.

Of any species. Anywhere.

Not just lovely, but kind. She'd been worried about my arm, even though her father was injured.

Sybil was different, warm.

I found time and time again I couldn't get her bright and perky smile out of my head. Maybe because I didn't want to.

I came around a dense copse of trees and was confronted by the sight of a spiky, serpentine creature with a vicious-looking stinger in its tail.

The Narrisiri had been a plague upon us until we'd made peace with the Puppet Master. Still, I decided to give the thing a wide berth, just in case.

The Narrisiri spotted me, and its frilled neck flared up, an intimidation display meant to keep me distant. Or so I thought. It slithered off the branch it had been resting on and made a beeline for me.

They were small creatures, but dangerous, so I hastened to move out of its path. But every time I changed position, it altered its trajectory to continue the charge. In a moment, it would have been right on top of me, so I did what I had to do.

I slung the assault rifle off my shoulder and held it at waist height. Just one squeeze of the trigger sent a three-round burst into the Narrisiri's path. But the stupid thing just kept on coming.

It was almost in striking distance when I took off the kid gloves. I sent another short burst of fire its way, only this time I aimed to kill. A moist popping sound accompanied an explosion of spikes and scales as the creature was torn asunder by bullets.

No sooner had I celebrated my victory to myself than I noticed three more of the creatures coming at me, bending the foliage aside as they came in for the attack. My lips peeled back in a snarl, and I took aim again. Three bursts went outward, and three more of the spiked serpents exploded into goo.

I slapped a new clip into my weapon as I turned this way and that, searching for more enemies. A hissing, liquid sound sizzled in the air behind me. I ducked, barely in time to avoid a stream of green venom as it squirted through the space where my head had been a second earlier.

I knew the sound, and the smell, of that particular venom. Peering through the gloom of the jungle, I spotted a seven-foot-tall tree with spindly limbs tipped by razor-sharp leaves.

A stained knothole on its trunk dripped with venom, and even as I took aim, it sent another deluge of toxic goo my way.

Something wasn't right, not at all. The Puppet Master was supposed to keep these things under control. Even as I dodged away from this newest attack, two more of the Sorvucs walked out of the undergrowth on their spindly roots.

I scrambled around the trunk of a thick tree as their venom streams hissed and bubbled through the air.

My finger snapped the weapon over to fully automatic. If these damn trees and snakes wanted a war, I was by god going to give them one.

With a thought, I flexed my scales to the surface and leaned my upper torso out around the stout trunk. I sent a barrage of deadly lead at one of the Sorvucs. My aim was true, and the trunk exploded into gooey shrapnel as my rounds found their mark. I managed to duck back behind my cover just before another hissing stream of venom hit the trunk where I'd been a second earlier.

The damn things were moving fast. They were nearly upon my position, so I beat a temporary retreat to another, larger tree.

The Sorvuc's leaves rasped against the rough bark, digging deep grooves as they lumbered—no pun intended—toward my new position.

I was done screwing around. Reaching down to my belt, I tore off a grenade and pulled the pin with my teeth. I sent the explosive twisting through the air to land at the feet-roots of the closest Sorvuc. The tree-thing recoiled from the impact, then continued on, undaunted. Right when its center mass was over the grenade, it exploded.

I ducked behind my cover as poison-covered bits of bark and weird, fleshy gobs that had no place in plant life decorated the jungle floor and canopy.

Two down, one to go. I charged around the other side of my cover and planted my feet. A guttural scream escaped my scarred and twisted mouth as I emptied the remainder of my clip at the last Sorvuc. It staggered about, oozing from dozens of smoking holes, before collapsing in a heap to shiver and die on the jungle floor.

I glanced around myself, making sure that I was finally bereft of foes. Nothing stirred other than the wind. The only thing I could hear was my heavy breathing and the pounding of my own heart.

I found a dense thicket to shelter in, holstered my weapon, and closed my eyes. My hand reached out to touch the living trees. My mind reached out to the ancient force which ruled—and was—the planet.

The Puppet Master had spoken to me in the past on

a single occasion. I was hoping he would remember and speak to me again.

Puppet Master. Can you hear me? Puppet Master.

I repeated the call several times. Then I felt a stirring in the front of my mind, a sort of prickly sensation which meant that the Puppet Master was trying to connect our minds.

A sudden rush nearly swept me off my feet. For a moment I could feel myself connected to the planet, as if I could feel every leaf, vine, and burrowing root.

Then the sensation left me, replaced by a presence, a consciousness, sharing my brain with me.

You are Cazak.

Yeah, yeah, I know the drill. What's the deal? How come your buddies are attacking me?

I got the feeling of my mind being searched.

Some of the children do not heed my call. I believe the Ancient Enemies to be responsible. Those under their thrall roam my jungles. I was forced to build a dome over one of your quake stations to protect it from their depredations. There are a number of humans as well as your people caught under the dome. I have just informed the one you know as Rouhr about that, as well.

So, you're saying there's nothing you can do? Thanks, I guess.

Your anger is understandable. I sense great turmoil in you, that—

I forcibly broke the contact, shoving him out of my mind. Anger surged through me.

I couldn't fight the Ancient Enemies, all I could do was hurt the innocent life forms they'd taken over.

And not even the Puppet Master, with powers that beggared the imagination, was going to be able to help me.

SYBIL

Dottie was kind enough to let me stay in her apartment in Nyheim while I waited.

If I understood correctly, it technically wasn't hers. It was made available to her whenever she was in the city for an extended period of time. I had the place to myself whenever Dottie was at work, which was most of the time.

She'd posted her schedule on the food storage unit so that I'd know when she was coming or going. She didn't stick to it, though. According to the schedule, she was supposed to be home at three this afternoon.

Around four, I got a message on my comm that she was going to work late again. I wasn't sure how often working late really meant spending time with her alien lover. Dottie knew I didn't judge her for falling in love with someone who wasn't human.

She could tell me if she was staying out with her man. Knowing Dottie, she either thought she was sparing me from feeling left out or she really was working late. If I had one-tenth of her work ethic, my dad wouldn't get so mad at me.

I paced the living space for the millionth time that day. I felt like I was going to jump right out of my skin. Nothing was worse than being cooped up like this.

If I were home and everything was normal, I'd be out on the town. I had a talent for sniffing out a good time.

I didn't want a good time right now. I just wanted a slightly better time. Even if I walked out the front door and stepped into the party of the century, I wouldn't be able to enjoy myself. Not with my dad locked up like a criminal.

I thought about calling Vidia, the mayor of Nyheim. She and I had met a few times over the course of her political career. I wasn't sure what my dad thought of her.

He was always polite when they talked, but that was how politics worked. He could hate her guts but would still shake her hand.

Vidia seemed nice. The people who weren't part of

that anti alien nonsense seemed to like her a lot. Maybe she could do me a favor and transfer my dad to a more comfortable place.

The least I could do was arrange for him to get better pillows and blankets. Maybe a better-quality sleeping mat, too. And some music. Dad liked music. A couple of datapads filled with stories and biographies wouldn't hurt, either.

I was about to call Vidia's office when I realized it was after seven. She probably wasn't there. I decided to send her a message instead.

Feeling a tiny bit accomplished, I decided to go out. I had no intention of partying or even getting a drink. I just needed to get out of this apartment for a little while. I wasn't familiar with Nyheim. I might as well do a little exploring while I was here.

I bundled myself up in a thick winter coat, tugged on my gloves, and stepped into a pair of Dottie's snow boots. I hadn't brought anything with me that was ideal for walking through snow. I could use the navigation chip built into my comm unit to find food, but in the end, I decided against it.

I'd rather stumble across something naturally. It was more fun that way, and I could use a small win.

Any kind of win at all.

When I stepped out into the city streets, the sky was

lit up with brilliant shades of orange, pink, and dusty purple. I couldn't see the actual sunset, the city's buildings were too tall. Seeing fractured reflections of the sky in every one of the city's windows was just as good as a full sunset.

Snow fell lightly, catching on my hair and eyelashes as I walked in a random direction.

I thought I'd feel more excitement. The idea of exploring a new city unsupervised would've appealed to me a few days ago, before dad got sick. I didn't think sick was the right word for what'd happened to him, but it sounded better than possessed.

I was supposed to be looking for food, or at least paying attention to where I was going, but I couldn't take my eyes off the sky. I stepped into the street without realizing, just as a zooming hovercar came around the corner.

I realized it was coming, but for some reason, I couldn't react quickly enough. Every fiber of my being was telling me to hold still or curl up.

A large hand wrapped around my bicep and yanked me back onto the paved walk. The driver of the hovercar made a rude gesture as he drove by.

"Wow." My legs shook as my body finally caught up to the situation. "That was a close call. I don't know what's wrong with me. Thanks for your help."

I turned to face my rescuer. To my surprise, I knew him.

"Cazak!" He didn't look at me. He kept his stony gaze fixed on some point over my head. "What are you doing here?"

Dumb question. Nyheim was his general's base of operations. I knew that, but I couldn't seem to act sensibly around him.

"Be more careful." He didn't say anything else. He just shoved his hands deep into his pockets and started walking away.

What the hell?

"Hey, wait up!" I had to jog to keep up with his long strides. I knew he could hear me. He was just ignoring me.

"Excuse me!" I said too loudly when I finally caught up to him. He didn't react, so I reached out and grabbed his arm. He didn't like that, but it made him stop walking, so I considered it a win.

"What's your problem?" I asked.

"I just saved your life. I don't have a problem," he muttered.

"You're acting like you wish that hovercar had run me over."

"That's not true."

"Yes, it is. Did I do something to offend you? If I

have, please tell me what I did. I promise I didn't mean it. I say stuff without thinking sometimes." I knew I was rambling, but I didn't care.

"You haven't offended me," he replied. I let out a frustrated groan.

"Then what did I do to make you so mad?" I exclaimed.

"I'm not mad."

"Do you just not like me? I don't think that's fair, since you don't know me."

"I have no opinion of you."

"Wow." I took a step back and folded my arms over my chest. "That's even worse than not liking me. Why did you save me since you clearly don't care?"

"I never said I don't care," he said. "And having no opinion of someone, and standing by while they get run down, are two completely different things."

"So, you're only obeying some kind of moral code?"

"I'm a soldier. Moral codes are our lives."

"That's not true. Soldiers follow orders against their moral codes all the time."

"General Rouhr's a good leader with good morals. I find it's not often an issue," he shrugged.

"You're getting off topic. Or are you trying to annoy me so I'll go away."

"I'm not trying to annoy you."

"If you want to be left alone, just say so."

When he didn't say anything, I smiled.

"We should go somewhere warmer and talk."

"About what?" he asked.

"Nothing. Everything. Anything."

"It's not possible to do all three." At that point, I was pretty sure he was trying to get under my skin.

"If you truly, in your heart of hearts, want me to leave you alone just say so. I'll go away."

"Heart of hearts? I only have one. So do humans. What are you talking about?"

"I'm not hearing you tell me to go away," I pressed.

"Why do you want to talk to me in the first place?"

"Because you've been helpful through this ordeal with my father. It seems only right that I take the time to get to know you better."

"So, this grand gesture stems from a false sense of obligation."

"Why are you being so difficult? You don't want to talk to me. You don't want to not talk to me. You're making everything ten times harder than it happens to be and I don't understand why. If you have any decency, will you please just agree to talk to me?"

"You're really fired up." A smirk tugged at the corner of his mouth.

"Yes, I am," I admitted. "So, what do you say?"

He stood in silence for several tense minutes.

"Sure. We can talk."

"Great. Let's get out of the snow. Any suggestions?"

"Yeah, I know a place." Without another word, he turned and started walking at a brisk pace.

"Yeah, that's fine," I said under my breath. "I'm up for a jog."

CAZAK

There had been many times that week that I'd fantasized about taking Sybil out to dinner. However, none of them had begun with her being angry at me.

The walk from where we'd bumped into each other to the restaurant seemed interminably long. Instead of walking like friends, or something closer, we moved like angry cats.

Not quite looking at each other, but still keeping pace over the snow-strewn streets of Nyheim.

"Wait." Sybil slowed to a stop and pointed at a sign over a cozy little restaurant. It depicted a human word I wasn't familiar with. "Let's eat here. I've been dying for some pasta."

"Pasta?" My mouth formed around the unusual word. "Is that some kind of fruit?"

Sybil chuckled, though I could tell she was still annoyed with me.

"Not hardly. Come on, my treat."

I remembered vaguely that I was supposed to pay, but it's not like we were on a real date. I followed her into the restaurant's warm interior.

Black and white floor tiles, polished to a gleam, reflected the overhead lights. Each of the small tables had a red and white checkered tablecloth draped over their square surfaces. Savory smells emanated from the kitchen area, causing my mouth to water.

A square-jawed human with a pot belly smeared a greasy rag over the counter. He flashed us a smile with some of his teeth missing, but seemed friendly enough.

"Two?" He didn't bat an eye at the sight of a human and an alien together. But when I turned my head and he saw my scarred face, his eyes briefly widened. He pulled himself together handily, though, and made no mention of it as he led us to a table in the corner.

Sybil settled into a seat opposite my own, and I had a hard time not staring at her. I'd spent so much time thinking about her, the fact that we were alone, together, about to have a normal meal, seemed somehow surreal.

In the warm air of the restaurant, I could breathe in

her scent, just enough to tide me over for weeks of daydreams.

Enough for me to realize she might never be mine, but I would always be hers.

We opened our menus and stared at the written words without reading them for several minutes, until she sighed and closed her own.

"All right, let's just get it out in the open." Sybil leaned on her elbows and stared at me intently. "What is your problem? Why have you been so, so distant and cold toward me? Do you just not like humans?"

I frowned, and set down my own menu.

"I don't have a problem with humans at all."

"Then it is something personal about me?"

"No, not at all. You're terrific—that is, I don't have any problems with you as a person." I coughed and cleared my throat, trying not to meet her gaze. "The truth is, I was just trying to protect you."

"Protect me?" She leaned back in her seat and fixed me with a stern glare. I got the feeling I had said something to offend her. "Protect me from what, my own bad decisions?"

"Ah, no." I shook my head and drained half my glass of water to give myself a moment to think. "Not that. I just—there are a lot of people who would give you a hard time just being seen with an alien, let alone eating dinner with one."

"What kinds of people do you mean?"

I was taken aback by her tone. Sybil didn't seem angry, not with me, but there was definite tension in her manner.

"You know, people. Your family, your fancy friends, the anti-alienists, you name it. There're plenty of folks who take exception to the *Vengeance* crew just being here, let alone fraternizing with humans."

"I see." Her eyes grew narrow, and she leaned over the table while staring me square in the eyes. "Well, as far as I'm concerned, if any of those people has a problem with it, they can kiss my ass."

My mouth went slack as I absorbed her words. Kiss her ass? Really? I would have expected a high society, spoiled rich girl like herself to be a stalwart of conformity.

After all, the nail that sticks out in the upper class tends to get hit, or so the saying goes.

But slowly it dawned on me that Sybil was dead serious. I realized then and there that, as infatuated as I'd been with her beauty, I had greatly underestimated her character. That fact made me want her more than I ever had before.

A grin broke out on my face before I could stop it. The thought of Sybil telling one of her high society chums to kiss her ass was amusing, but even more so, it was validating.

For a brief moment, I didn't feel so self-conscious sitting there with her.

Sybil took a deep breath, paused, and looked at me with meaning. I knew whatever came out of her mouth next, it would pertain to a dicey subject.

"If you don't mind my asking, Cazak, how did you get that scar?"

My scar. For the first time while we were talking, I had forgotten about it.

Now there I was, sitting there with a stupid grin on my face that was only going to stretch and deform my already scarred face in bizarre ways.

Without thinking about it, I cupped a hand on my chin to hide as much of it as I could.

"You—you don't really want to hear about that, do you?" My voice seemed as weak as my knees. I was better equipped to deal with people and monsters that wanted to kill me than eating dinner with a lovely young woman.

"I'm very interested, if you want to share." Sybil shrugged and picked up her menu. "But you don't have to tell me if you don't want to."

I hesitated for a moment, watching her read the menu. Should I tell her the story? It would mean letting her know about what a dumbass I'd been when I was younger.

"No, it's all right. I'll tell you."

Sybil lowered her menu and stared at me with her enchanting dark eyes. I nearly lost my nerve, but then I rolled into my story.

"So, when I was a young hothead full of the cry of the warrior, I felt like I could take on the world. I was second in my class at hand-to-hand combat, right behind my cousin Jalok, and it was next to guaranteed that I'd be entering the military after I finished my compulsory education."

"Wait, was this on your homeworld?"

I nodded.

"Yes, before the Xathi invasion. Anyway, me and some of my troopmates headed into a rougher tavern. We'd already had a lot to drink, when another drunk soldier barreled right into me and made me spill my drink all over my shirt."

I gave a deep sigh, and looked her square in the eyes.

"Now, it was completely his fault, of course, but I could have reacted better than I did. When he stared at me, all bleary eyed, I could have just let it go, but I didn't. Instead, I called him a stupid skrell and demanded a full apology AND that he pay to have my clothes cleaned."

"Oh wow." Sybil waved away the waiter since we weren't ready to order yet. "I'm guessing he didn't take that too well?"

"You're guessing right. He insulted me, I kept

insulting him, and pretty soon, my troopmates were egging me on to fight him. Except Jalok. I don't know why he was the voice of reason that night, but he was. I should have listened to him and just walked away."

I went to take a drink of water, but my glass was empty. Sybil wordlessly pushed her own glass across the table, her gaze rapt with attention. I took a drink and continued my tale.

"Well, let me tell you, there's a big difference between a real fight and a sparring match. The soldier was drunk, but he could still move fast. It seemed like I couldn't really take it all in at once. One second, he was standing there and we were squaring up, and the next, he reached out and blasted me in the jaw.

"Neither of us had our scales out at that point. It's considered a, well, if you'll pardon the phrase, a 'pussy move' to pop your scales in anything but a deadly fight. So, my jaw was aching, but I reached out and smacked him with a right cross to the temple. He folded like a blanket, and I figured he was down and out."

I took another drink of water and fingered the side of my face with the scar.

"Unfortunately, he picked up a bottle off the floor, smashed it against a table leg, and came up slashing with what was left. I didn't have time to react. He caught me on the side of the head and...well, you see the result. Guess I lost my ear as a lesson to make sure I listen to the voice of reason next time."

"That's quite a story." Sybil pursed her lips, then reached across the table.

"What are you doing?" My voice had a tremble to it as her fingers stretched toward my face.

"Shh. It's all right."

Sybil's fingers gently stroked the side of my face, running through the deep grooves and furrows of my scar. I gasped when she traced a line around the hole where my ear used to be, and closed my eyes, expecting her to recoil with horror at any second.

She didn't, though. I opened my eyes to find her smiling at me, nothing at all akin to disgust in her gaze.

My heart started pounding in my chest, and I wondered if I'd died and gone to paradise.

SYBIL

I knew Cazak wasn't as big of an ass as he'd tried to come off as. The more I talked to him, the more I believed that he wasn't trying to come off as an ass at all. The way he reacted when I touched his scar was...sweet.

"Ready to go?" he asked once I'd polished off my second slice of chocolate myberri pie. It was my favorite. I hadn't had it since I was a kid. I couldn't believe this place served it.

"I want a third slice," I declared.

Cazak's eyes widened. I couldn't tell if he was impressed or horrified.

"I'm kidding," I laughed. "I'm so full I don't think I can walk."

"I'll carry you if need be." His eyes shone with a

gentleness that made my heart do strange things. I wanted to reach out and touch his face again.

He paid the bill before I could reach into my purse.

"You didn't have to pay for everything. I had more dessert than you did," I protested.

"Don't worry about it. I'm happy to feed you after all you've had to deal with."

"When you put it that way." I shrugged and pulled myself out of the booth. My overstuffed stomach begged me to lie down and take a long nap.

A server appeared with a to-go bag filled with food cartons.

"What's that?"

"Something for you and Dottie to snack on in the middle of the night," Cazak said. "Just in case you can't get back here anytime soon. There are two slices of that pie in here."

"I don't know what to say," I gushed. "Thank you."

I reached to take the bag from him, but the smell of food made my stomach churn.

"I'll grab that from you in a minute, okay?" I placed my hand on my stomach and groaned.

"Walking will help," Cazak smirked.

"Walking sounds like hell." We stepped out onto the street. It was snowing harder now, but not by much. The wind picked up. It blew right through my winter coat. I wrapped my arms around myself and tried not to shiver.

"Do you want my coat? It's thicker than yours." Cazak's coat was still draped over his arm.

"No, you should wear it," I insisted. "I don't want you to get chilly."

"I'm not chilly," he replied with a laugh. "I'm nearly frozen, but I'm tough."

"This town gets pretty miserable in the winter," I admitted.

"Take the jacket." He didn't wait for me to answer before wrapping the jacket over my shoulders. Too cold to care about being polite anymore, I pulled it on. It was massive on me, but I didn't care. It was warm and smelled like Cazak.

I had to fight the urge to lift the sleeve to my nose and take a deep breath.

"I'll give it back once I can feel my fingertips again," I said.

"No need. I'm walking you home. You can give it back to me when you're in Dottie's apartment with the heater running."

"You don't have to do that," I protested, though I was secretly thrilled.

Cazak rolled his eyes and jerked his head in the direction of Dottie's apartment. This time, he didn't walk so fast that I had to jog to keep up. He let me set the pace.

"An hour and a half ago you were bullying me into talking to you," he said as we walked. "Now, the thought of causing the slightest inconvenience to me seems to put you off."

"I am a woman of many contradictions," I shrugged. "That's just how I am."

"I'm sure that makes for an interesting lifestyle."

"Not really." I looked at the ground and frowned. "I go to a lot of parties and social events because I have nothing better to do. I wouldn't call them exciting, though. I'd call them a way to pass the time."

"Well, I can't promise a party, but I can promise stimulating conversation if you're interested."

"That sounds better than any party I can think of." I smiled up at him.

"You're nicer than you let on," he replied. "Why is that?"

"I think it's a defense mechanism or something," I parroted what one of my psychologists once told me. "Since my dad is who he is, people gravitate toward me. They don't really care about me or even want to be my friend. They just want whatever perks they think I can get them. If I'm mean right off the bat, I scare all those people off before they can take advantage of me."

"I can imagine why that's an effective coping

mechanism," Cazak nodded. "Sounds awful and exhausting."

"It is. Hence the partying. Fun distraction." I didn't know why I was telling him all this. I never got that personal with anyone. Dottie's the only other person that knew I'm not the crazy party-girl everyone thought I was, but even she didn't know about the coping mechanism theory.

We reached Dottie's apartment. I fumbled with the key at the door.

"Let me," Cazak offered. "I'm sure your hands are freezing."

"Just a touch." I passed the key to him and he swiftly opened the door. Once inside, I shrugged off his coat and handed it back to him.

"You can keep it on until you warm up," he offered.

I walked over to the climate control panel on the wall and turned the heater all the way up.

"I'll be warmed up in a moment. Let me know if it gets too warm for you." Hot air blasted through the vents around the apartment. I gestured to the couch. "Make yourself at home."

Cazak took a seat on the couch while I paced the living space, rubbing my hands together and trying not to make it look obvious that I was still freezing.

"I'm going to make some hot tea. Do you want any?"

"No, thank you. But a glass of water would be appreciated."

I put the kettle on and filled a glass up with water. I sat on the couch beside Cazak while I waited for my water to boil.

"You know something?" I asked. "You're nicer than you let on, too."

"You can say the same thing about most soldiers," he said after draining his glass. "I don't have a fancy coping mechanism for it. Or at least I don't think I do. It's easier to get the job done when people think you're mean. The scar helps."

"You seemed shocked when I touched your scar at the restaurant," I blurted without thinking. Thankfully, the shrill cry of my teakettle gave me a way out. I prepped my tea and returned to the couch, thinking my awkward statement could be forgotten.

"No one's touched my scar before," he said as if I hadn't gotten up at all.

"I'm sorry. I don't always think before I do things."

"I'm not upset," he smiled reassuringly. "I'm just curious as to why you wanted to touch it."

"I like it." I winced on my words. "I know, that sounds weird. I like scars in general. I think they're sexy, but they also tell stories about the people who bear them."

"I suppose you're right." Cazak looked like he

wanted to say something else, but couldn't find the words.

"Are you okay?" I put my hand on his arm.

"Yes." A smile twitched at the corner of his mouth. "I just want to kiss you and I'm not sure how to go about asking permission."

"Permission granted." With a laugh, I leaned in and pressed my lips to his. His kiss was warm and soft, but deep enough for me to lose myself in.

There was something so safe and comforting about his presence. The thought of being without him was unbearable.

I wrapped my arms around his neck and pulled myself closer to him. He pulled me onto his lap and held me tight. I could spend eternity right here, just like this.

We kissed until my lips were sore and swollen. I stood up and extended a hand to him, asking silently. He took my hand and stood.

Together, we walked to the small set of stairs that led up to the bedrooms. I didn't turn on any of the lights.

Once in the smaller of the two bedrooms, the one I'd stored my things in, I let Cazak take over.

He stood me in the center of the room in the dark. With the utmost care, he undressed me piece by piece, until I was completely naked. I'd never been so exposed like that, so vulnerable to another person.

Then he allowed me to do the same to him. In the darkness, I ran my hands over every inch of his body like I wanted to memorize it.

I slid my fingers over his chest and up his neck to the side of his face. He didn't move when I softly traced his scar with the tip of my finger; it was such a sign of acceptance, of feeling comfortable with me. When I finished, he cupped my face in his hands and crushed his mouth to mine.

This time, our kiss was streaked with fire and passion.

He backed me up until my knees hit the bed. I fell backward, trusting him to not let me fall too far. With a soft thud, I landed onto the mattress, the slight springs cushioning my fall. Instantly, he was on top of me, his body pressed tightly against mine. It wasn't just his body that felt incredible against me, though, it was the weight of him.

I was pinned, immobilized by him.

Yet I was content in that, my heart skipping a beat every time he left a featherlight kiss on my skin. What stirred me most of all about his kisses, however, was how, with each touch of his lips, his hard shaft flexed against my thigh. I could feel how passionately he wanted to be inside me. Nothing except the exploration of every inch of me would suffice.

Moaning into his kisses, my face rose up even higher to meet those soft lips of his. Instinctively, I spread myself wider for him. In response, Cazak stroked his hands down my navel and to just above my mound. The time he waited before dipping his fingers past the edge and between my swollen pussy lips felt like forever.

The moment he touched my hidden folds, their slick, intricate pleats enticing him in, I felt my head swim with giddiness.

I wanted this more than words could say. Even the signs my body were giving didn't seem adequate enough to convey my lustful desire for him.

"Please... Cazak..."

I didn't need to say anything more. Instantly, he knew what I needed, his body moving to fit into the mold I'd created for the two of us. As he re-positioned himself, I felt the oozing head of his cock brush against me, the tautness of his muscle leaving a slick trail as it went. I wanted to feel his seed inside me, for him to fill me with it — being teased like that almost felt cruel.

As always, Cazak knew what to do.

His hand still between my thighs, my throbbing clit aching from every touch he made, I trembled as he massaged me.

Satisfied that I was worked up enough, Cazak reached further down to my entrance, his fingertips beginning to open me up, stretching me so that I could accommodate his enormous size.

"You feel incredible... and I still haven't discovered every part of you yet," he whispered, his voice husky.

Hearing him so unsettled, so mesmerized by lust, sent my body racing. Reacting to the idea of him entering me, gooseflesh mottled my skin, and I let out a low moan.

Slowly, he slid two fingers inside me.

I moaned as I writhed, the feeling of him pushing deeper into me, even with just his fingers, was almost too great to bear. I became frenzied, hungry for more — nothing short of his cock filling me would do. I needed it now.

I lifted my head to look him deep in the eyes. Looking through half-closed eyes, I silently implored him to use more than just his fingers. A delighted grin greeted me, one which held a playful smugness. He was enjoying how he was making me feel.

At first, I felt like the odd one out, as if I was the only one savoring this moment. But when I bucked up into his fingers to take more of them inside, I felt his engorged cock against me.

He was struggling just as much as I was.

Feeling Cazak's knuckles deep inside, I could feel

every slight movement, every curve of his fingers. When they located my G-spot and started to knead, I bit down on my lower lip to stop from crying out with ecstasy, it felt so good.

Wave upon wave rocked my curves as he stroked in a come-hither motion, surrounded by the walls of my tight pussy.

When I began spasming, my orgasm imminent, I tried to stop myself from coming undone. I didn't want it to end here — there was more for us to experience. However, Cazak gave me a knowing look, his fingers never ceasing their skilled exploration.

"Don't hold back," he begged me, his eyes locked onto mine.

"But... I want... you inside of me..." I managed to pant out, struggling to not spill my juices all over his hand. To that he replied with a wider smile than before.

"I don't intend this night to end without feeling that, Sybil."

In knowing that, I finally allowed myself to let go. It was unlike anything I'd ever felt or dreamed of. I'd had lovers before, but never so experienced in lovemaking that I forgot everything surrounding me except myself and my lover.

Shuddering around him, my walls clenching his fingers with every wave of my climax, I cried out for him. I lost myself to a moment that would stay with me even if that was where our time together came to an end. No matter the future, that was what I'd always remember of Cazak.

Before I finished pouring myself onto his fingers, he was already stealing them away from me. Watching with hazy, lust-filled eyes and curiosity, I saw him raise his fingers to his mouth and lick.

"Mmmmm, you taste amazing," he purred.

My already flushed skin turned an even darker shade of crimson. But, having seen him lap up my slickness in such a way, I was already desperate to have more of him. And Cazak was happy to oblige.

Using both his hands, he lifted my legs and slung them over his shoulders, my body folding into place. Then, with my pussy spread before him, he positioned himself right at my dripping wet entrance.

The moment the broad head of his cock connected with my skin, I shook. So did he.

Inch by inch, he pushed his way inside, the way it felt as he filled me was a pleasure I can't find words to describe.

"Sybil... you're beautiful..."

"Shut up and... kiss me..." I ordered him, my urges taking over as I pushed up against his hips.

He matched me with his thrusts. Hard and slow, he drew back only to pound forward into me; it was a steady rhythm, but the force behind it shook me to my core.

Cazak had such command of himself and, in turn, of me. As he took me toward the edge of euphoria again, I strove to take him there with me. We both needed this, to come together as one.

His body peeling away from mine, I relished feeling him glide back into me right to the hilt. There were no half measures, nothing left unexplained.

What we needed from one another was what we got. An endless moment in time of him and me working toward a climax that everyone in the building would hear.

They could probably hear my passion already, my moans loudly ringing around the room.

As he slammed into me faster, I felt the rush of excitement tremble inside me. At the same time, I felt him twitch. That was followed by more spasms, his fluid shooting out. He was an uncorked bottle, the flow unstoppable until the pressure was depleted. As he flooded my slick walls, my orgasm gushed to meet him.

We took turns chasing each other over the edge of the deepest pleasures I've ever known. Never before had I felt so much at one time. I simultaneously felt like I was drowning, flying, and burning. He pushed me to new edges until I could only say one word.

His name.

CAZAK

She said yes.

There I had been, feeling awkward and inadequate and like a total ass, and I'd actually asked Sybil if I could kiss her. It was a lame, newbie type of move, or so Jalok would have said.

But it had just felt right, like the right thing to say, and Sybil had said yes. Yes, she didn't mind kissing me, even with my scarred face. Even though I was an alien, and she was likely condemning herself to ridicule and prejudice just by being with me.

The feel of her full, soft lips against my own still glowed in my memory as I sat there in a chair watching her sleep. I think, in a lot of ways, I was still high on that first kiss, even though we'd gone much, much further.

I was going to have to apologize to Jalok for all the hard times I'd given him over having a human girlfriend. For that matter, I owed an apology to Sk'lar, too, but he was such a tightass, I wasn't about to offer one.

The memory of her skin sliding against my own was one that I would always treasure. Thank goodness our bodies were sexually compatible. Sybil certainly hadn't been the least bit afraid of my cock, that was for certain.

Her body was every bit as soft as it appeared, and I remember thinking how lucky I was that I'd gotten to experience it. Never in a million years would I have believed that a lovely woman like her would ever let a scarred-up old soldier like me even touch her, but truth is stranger than fiction sometimes.

Sybil rolled over onto her side, a bit of her dark hair hanging over her face, and snored softly. Carefully, with great gentleness, I reached out and lifted the hair away from her sleeping eyes so I could still see her loveliness. Her warm breath tickled the back of my hand when I moved near her nostrils. My eyes ran over the curves of her body, ill-concealed beneath the thin silk sheet draped over her naked form.

I returned to my seat and kept watching her sleep. If I'd have heard someone describe doing such to me, I would have thought they were a total creep, but now I understood the feeling. It wasn't about dominance or control, but about trust. Sybil trusted me enough to be totally vulnerable to me. Her slumber proved that she believed I was a good man, not someone who would ever hurt her.

My jaw set hard. I wouldn't ever hurt her, or allow her to be hurt. Something flashed through my mind, a thought that if the Ancient Enemies took over one of our minds, I might be forced to cause her harm, but I refused to consider it. If there were any way possible to resist the Ancient Enemies, I resolved to do it.

The sound of the front door opening made me start. So soon after thinking about mental possessions by incorporeal beings, I suppose I was on high alert. When I heard Dottie and Jalok speaking, I relaxed.

For a moment, I considered waking Sybil, but one look at how peaceful she seemed dismissed the notion. Since I didn't want to wake her or disturb her in any way, I dressed with the utmost caution so as not to make any noise.

Once I was suitably modest, I paused to consider her sleeping form one more time. I caressed her hip through the sheet, gently so as not to wake her, then opened the door and walked into the living space of Dottie's apartment.

Dottie and Jalok sat in the den, both occupying the sofa. They were smiling at each other, but those smiles faded into confusion when they realized it was me, not Sybil, who had exited the guest bedroom.

"Cazak?" Jalok looked me up and down, his eyes doing calculations. "What are you doing here...oh, you dog. Congratulations."

I couldn't help feeling a bit abashed at his words. I stared out the window, scratched the back of my head, and laughed nervously.

"Oh, my goodness." Dottie laughed, and nodded as if in approval. "Well, I wasn't expecting this, but I suppose I should have been."

"Why is that?" Both Jalok and I asked the question at the same time.

"Because of the way Sybil kept asking about Cazak. And the way her eyes would shine whenever his name came up." Dottie turned her gaze on me and beamed a smile. "Basically, she's been crushing on you hardcore ever since the first day you met."

"Really?" I shook my head in disbelief. "That's hard to swallow."

"I know, right?" Jalok laughed. "Who would have thought a high-class human like Sybil would let an ugly ass grunt like you even touch her."

His words stung, but I tried to keep it off my face. I must have flinched or something, though, because Dottie quickly came to my defense.

"Cazak is not ugly. He's actually quite handsome."

"No way." Jalok and I spoke again in unison. We were going to have to stop doing that before it got weird.

"Yes, way. His burnt orange skin really makes his lovely eyes pop. I'd do him, if I wasn't already involved."

I couldn't stifle a laugh while Jalok sputtered.

"Oh, calm down, honey, you know you're the only scaly alien for me."

Dottie kissed him on the cheek, and I felt warm watching them interact. Not jealous, not anymore. Just warm.

"Still, though." Jalok shook his head, staring at me and at the closed bedroom door. "Cazak and Sybil. Never would have seen it coming."

"Well, I should have." Dottie grinned up at me. "Sybil's not the pampered princess you think she is. Ah, that is, she is, and she isn't."

"Perhaps you could explain that statement." Jalok jutted his chin at me. "Because Cazak looks confused."

"Don't throw me under the bus, cousin."

"Stop it, both of you. Look, Sybil has been around politics all her life. That means that she's been around politicians all her life, too. Her dad is an alright guy—when he's not possessed by ancient incorporeal aliens, of course—but it takes a certain, ah, veneer to be in politics."

"You mean you have to be full of shit to win."

"Shut up, Jalok." Dottie sighed and looked at me and shrugged. "Yeah, basically he's right, though. Sybil has been around men her whole life who do nothing but present their best side and hide anything that might besmirch their public image. Someone like you, Cazak, is so much more honest about who you are. It doesn't matter if you aren't refined, or cultured. What matters is that you're a good guy, and she could sense that about you right from the get-go."

I couldn't help but smile at her words, but I was curious about Sybil, too. There was still a lot of things I didn't know about her at that point in our relationship.

"I guess I didn't realize the type of woman she really was at first."

"No, you didn't." Dottie stuck out her tongue at me. "I'd tell you all about her, but I think you should enjoy the experience of finding out yourself. Trust me, you're not going to regret getting to know her. She's a lot more solid a person than most people give her credit for, and smart as a whip, too."

"Oh, come on, now." Jalok nudged her with his knee. "There must be something you can tell him. Give the poor guy a clue, will you?"

"Hmm." Dottie looked up at the ceiling and smiled smugly. "I guess I could tell you her favorite color is sunset orange. A lot like your skin color."

That put a smile on my face. Dottie laughed warmly

and Jalok shook his head, though he was smiling, too. I got the impression my cousin was quite proud of me in that moment.

And I found myself wanting to know more about Sybil. My infatuation, my crush if you will, may have been fulfilled but now it had been replaced by a deeper, if calmer, need to know her inside and out. Sybil intrigued me on new levels that I hadn't thought possible. She was clearly more than just a pretty face.

The three of us chatted some more, which mostly consisted of Jalok and me trying to glean more tidbits of information from Dottie. Sybil's friend remained tight-lipped, however. I do think she enjoyed the power play dynamics of having information we did not.

Eventually we were interrupted, as I was called in for duty. Sybil still slumbered in the bedroom, but at Dottie's suggestion, I penned her a note. I tried not to be too over the top, but I made sure to tell her that I wanted to see her again that evening.

How could I not want more of her?

She was amazing. She was sweetness and fire.

And she was mine.

SYBIL

Since the spare room I used didn't have many windows, there was a light that simulated the rising sun. I woke up to the artificial light, feeling rested. There was a pleasant ache in my limbs that felt sore in the best possible way when I stretched.

I rolled over, expecting to find Cazak in bed next to me. Instead, I found an expanse of blankets and sheets.

"Cazak?" I lifted my head and looked around the small space as if he could be hiding behind my minuscule pile of laundry.

Sadness welled up in me. This wasn't the first time I'd woken up to an empty bed after a night of fun. I was expecting something different with Cazak, though.

I told myself it was fine. I'd done the casual thing before. Usually, I insisted on it. But last night, I swear I felt something deep and meaningful. I'd never felt anything like that before. Waking up to find him gone wasn't a relief. It was a punch in the gut.

I wrapped the sheet around myself, intending to sneak into the bathroom, when something clattered to the floor. It was a pocket-sized datapad. It didn't belong to me. I'd never seen Dottie with anything like it, either.

I picked it up and powered it on. It opened to a short note.

Last night was perfect. I've got to head into work early today and didn't want to wake you. I hope to see you later. This evening, if you're free?

Cazak

Sadness seeped out of my body and was replaced with a warm, bubbly feeling. I knew he wouldn't just leave like that. I placed the datapad on the small nightstand for safekeeping and walked to the bathroom.

I could hear Dottie milling about in the common area. Once I'd showered and dressed, I went downstairs to join her.

"Hey, sleepyhead," she said with a knowing look in her eyes. "Did you have a good night?"

"Why do you ask?" I made no effort to look coy.

"I ran into Cazak as he was going on duty."

"He didn't wake you up, did he?" I wasn't ashamed that he'd stayed over, but Dottie was kind enough to offer me her spare room. I'd feel terrible if I'd caused a disturbance.

"No, I was already up." She waved her hand dismissively. "We had a nice little chat before he took off."

"About what?"

"How great you are." Dottie affectionately bumped me with her shoulder. "He really likes you."

"He said that?"

"Not in so many words, but it was written all over his face. Coffee?"

"Please."

Dottie poured a cup of steaming coffee and set it down in front of me. I took a long sip, even though it burned my tongue. When I set the cup down, I noticed Dottie was staring at me with a wide grin.

"What?"

"Is he good?" she asked.

"Very." I winked.

"Tell me everything." She leaned forward with a hungry look in her eyes. I was about to spill all of the dirty details when her comms unit went off. The indicator light on her comm flashed, too

"Hang on." Her brow furrowed as she answered. "This is Dottie."

I could faintly hear the voice of whoever was calling

her, but I couldn't make out any words. Dottie's face dropped.

"Right. Thank you." She disconnected the call, looking pale.

"What is it?" I asked.

"It's, um," she paused, "your dad."

The cup I held slipped from my hand and clattered onto the counter. It didn't tip over, but hot coffee sloshed everywhere. I barely felt the burn.

"What happened?"

"I'm not sure. The detention center said you needed to come down right away."

I wasted no time. I leaped to my feet and grabbed my coat from upstairs. I needed gloves. Where the hell were my gloves? I ended up half-running, half-stumbling down the stairs with mismatched gloves and only one boot. The other one had to be around there somewhere.

"Right there." Dottie pointed to the toe of my boot sticking out from under the sofa. How had it gotten there? It didn't matter. Dottie was ready to go by the time I pulled it on.

"You sure you're up for this?" she asked as we left the apartment.

"They said it was an emergency. He's my dad. It doesn't matter if I'm up for it."

I debated sending a message to Cazak to let him

know what was going on. I decided against it. He was working and didn't need the distraction. Besides, it might be nothing. I didn't want to worry him needlessly.

Dottie and I arrived at the detention center in record time. The receptionist sat at her desk, typing on her console. Luckily, no one else was there.

"We're here for subject K5825." Dottie rattled off my father's prison ID. It made me feel sick to hear him referred to as a number.

"Visiting hours don't start for another hour and a half," the receptionist said without looking up.

"This isn't a recreational visit," I clarified. "My friend received a page regarding my father. The mayor of Kaster."

"I didn't realize we were talking about that patient," she stammered. "Go right in."

A blaring alarm by the cellblock door screeched. A security guard opened it for us.

"Do you want me to go in with you?" Dottie asked.

"No," I replied. "I can handle this."

"I'll make sure guards are posted," she said.

"Thanks." I squeezed her hand and went through the open door. The guard who held the door open helped me find my father's cell.

I don't know what I was expecting. Maybe to find

him completely mad beyond recovery? Maybe to find that he'd ripped into a guard?

I wasn't expecting to find him sitting cross-legged on the floor of his cell with a serene smile on his face.

"We have someone monitoring the cell from the security station and two men will be posted by the door," the guard informed me as he let me into the cell.

"Is it safe?" I should've asked that sooner.

"Of course it is, honey," my dad said. "I'm perfectly fine."

I looked to the guard for confirmation. He nodded.

"You look confused. Come sit." Dad gestured to the floor in front of him. I sat down opposite him and crossed my legs to mirror his.

"Dottie received an alert. We were worried that something had happened."

"Nothing to worry about," my father waved his hand dismissively. "I'm glad you're here. I asked them to summon you."

"How are you doing, dad?" I asked.

"Have you seen where I live?" He looked around the small cell and laughed.

"I tried to make it more comfortable," I told him. "Turns out it's really hard to get feather pillows in here."

"I appreciate the effort." He sounded like his old self again. My heart swelled with relief, but I couldn't shake the sinking feeling that it wouldn't last. Why else would he still be in here?

"It's good to see you." My throat felt thick with tears I refused to shed.

"You, too, honey. You're looking well. Nyheim agrees with you, though I'm not surprised. I always knew you'd thrive in a bigger city. Kaster's too small for someone as large as life, like you."

"Kaster's not so bad," I shrugged. "Though it's been nice getting to spend time with Dottie. And there are way more restaurants here. I went to the best diner yesterday. It had our favorite pie."

"I hope you had an extra slice for me," he smiled.

"I did. And I took two more home." I decided not to mention Cazak.

"Do you remember when we special ordered that pie for your sixth birthday?"

"You foolishly thought ordering two would be enough," I laughed.

"I didn't count on you eating an entire pie by yourself."

"I was sick for three days."

"I know. I was the one cleaning up after you."

Mom was already gone by then. The grim reminder wiped the smile off my face.

"You're a lot like her, you know?" Dad said. "That

was her favorite pie, too. If she had been there, I know she would've eaten the other one all on her own."

"I'm glad she and I share the same pie-eating habits." Talking about her felt strange.

"You have a lot more of her in you than your insatiable hunger for pie. You have her drive, her energy. You got your good looks from me, though."

"Whatever you say," I rolled my eyes, thrilled to finally have somewhat of a normal conversation with him, despite still wondering why he had asked them to send for me. "I'm glad you're doing better, Dad."

"Me, too."

Hopefully, this nightmare was reaching its close.

"I should get going," I said after he and I talked for a while longer. I stood up. My legs ached from sitting on the floor for so long. I offered my hand to Dad, but he didn't take it. He looked up at me with a strange expression.

"You okay?" I asked, fearing the worst. I looked over my shoulder to make sure the guards were still in place in case Dad took a turn. They were.

"Before you go, I have to tell you something important."

CAZAK

The jungle spread out beneath us like a technicolor cloak as our shuttle skimmed through the air toward Aramita. Sakev, another Skotan like me, sat in the copilot seat, turning a rueful eye on me every time we hit turbulence.

"Damn it, Cazak, you do know how to fly one of these things, don't you?"

"Have we crashed?"

"No, but—"

"Then shut the skrell up. She's sluggish on account of, oh, I don't know, the several tons of food we're carrying in the cargo hold. Can't help it if I have to fly low enough, we're hitting the vertical wind shear."

"Vertical wind shear, my ass. You're just a shitty pilot."

"Man, maybe you should spend more time with Evie. You're a little uptight."

"Ha ha. Speaking of Evie, there's a human expression that goes like this; People who live in glass houses shouldn't throw stones."

"That just sounds like a good idea."

"Yeah, and it pertains to you. Or have you not been cozying up to a certain politician's daughter?"

"Whatever. It's not like I'm the one who's uptight."

"From what I heard transpired, that's not surprising. Just wait until you get deeper into the relationship. Then you'll discover it's not all wine and roses." He scowled, then his grin broke out. "But they're so very, very worth it."

I checked our telemetry and found, thankfully, that we were close to our destination.

"Setting in approach vector. Looks like the welcome wagon has been rolled out for us."

"More likely they're freaking hungry."

The landing pad loomed beneath us, complete with some ground crew prepared to unload our precious, if boring, cargo. Snowfall had been just as heavy here as elsewhere, but the high winds kept the concrete landing pad clean as a whistle. I brought the shuttle down in a gentle arc and settled her onto the landing pylons.

Unfortunately, a combination of high winds and my relative unfamiliarity with piloting a fully loaded cargo shuttle made the touchdown a bit rougher than necessary.

Sakev lurched around in his seat dramatically, but I'm pretty sure he was hamming it up.

"Watch it, I think you just gave me whiplash."

"Well, hearing your voice for the last several hours has given me tinnitus, so I guess we're even."

Sakev headed outside to supervise the unloading process. I had fun watching him shiver in the cold on my monitor. The shuttle sat higher on its suspension as the food was unloaded. I looked forward to flying it without the extra weight.

I decided to have a little fun while Sakev was still outside. I closed the entrance ramp and then 'forgot' to turn my comm on. He walked around, pounding on the hull for several minutes between shivers. Good times.

After about the tenth time he shouted 'I know you can hear me, damn it' I finally let the ramp down.

"Oh, hey, are you all done out there?"

"Fuck off. If I die of pneumonia, I'll never speak to you again."

Amid Sakev's bitching, I started up the shuttle's engines and we rose into the air. Our ascent was a bit extreme, as I still had the shuttle set up to lift heavy weights. My belly bottomed out and Sakev gripped his armrests for dear life.

"The hell is wrong with you?"

"Sorry. I've got it under control. We're all good now."

"Just don't make us crash. It's a long walk back to Nyheim."

"I'm not going to crash."

"Yeah, that's what they all say right before they crash."

I turned to face my fellow Skotan and jabbed a finger at him.

"Sakev, if I crash this shuttle, I'll buy you a round at the pub AND I'll kiss your ass."

"Promises, promises."

We sailed through the air, mostly just shooting the breeze without talking about anything too heavy. I did mention the situation at the quake station, and how the Puppet Master had to protect them from the hybrids lurking about in the woods. We were reporting the news up the chain as well, but the sooner the message was dispersed, the better.

"If you ask me, I'd rather be fighting the damn bugs than dealing with incorporeal beings you can't see or touch."

"Yeah, at least the Xathi made it obvious when they took over someone's mind."

"Did you know Tyehn had to kill a young mother during the Xathi invasion to protect her children?"

Sakev glanced at me sharply.

"No, I didn't."

"Yeah. He's pretty laid back about it all, but I can tell it actually bothers him a lot."

"Well, I can see that. Valorni aren't soldiers, like us Skotan."

"I don't think it has anything to do with that—"

The shuttle lurched violently in the air and an earsplitting explosion rang throughout the cabin amid the screeching of metal. Suddenly we were dipping hard to the right. I glanced at the myriad red lights flashing on my console and gritted my teeth.

"What the hell? Did you hit something?"

"No, something hit us. Artillery fire. The entire right-side stabilizer array is off line."

"Can you see what—"

The shuttle rocked again, and this time the cabin was penetrated. Our uniforms whipped into furrows and ridges from the air being sucked outside. I glanced back over my shoulder and saw twisted metal and gray skies.

"That took out our engines. We're deadweight." I checked the panel, but it was useless. "Brace for impact."

We had been hit near the site of the *Vengeance* crash, and the miles-long swath of slow regrowth which marked its passage. Considering who had taken up residence in its shadow, it wasn't hard to guess who'd attacked our shuttle.

The shuttle dropped out of the sky like a lead weight. With no wings to speak of, the craft had no means of lift and only our momentum kept us moving forward as well as down. Sakev and I braced ourselves as the shuttle dipped below the tree line. A rapid tattoo echoed through the cabin as the shuttle broke through branches on its way down.

We were jostled about roughly, but at the same time, I was grateful for the trees slowing us down. I tried to steer us away from the larger trunks, but without engines, there was little I could do. The entire left side of our chassis was sheared off by one of the knobby trees, and then the shuttle's belly smashed into the jungle floor. Upon impact, I felt a sharp pain in the roof of my mouth—I later found I had broken a bone in it, which I hadn't even thought possible—and I banged my forehead on the console pretty hard. Fortunately, both Sakev and I had our scales out, which prevented us from being maimed in the wreck.

Sakev seemed to have hurt his leg, and both of us were bleeding from tiny cuts and were generally banged up. We sat there groaning in misery for a moment as the shuttle's engines popped and smoked.

"Sakev, you alive?"

"Yeah." He coughed in the heavy smoke. "We can't stay here."

"I know. Are you able to send out a distress beacon?"

"Yeah, I think so."

"Good. Do that while I prep our meager weaponry."

"Weaponry?"

"Somebody shot us down on purpose. You think they're going to assume we died in the crash, or are they going to come and make sure?"

"If it was me, I'd come and be sure."

"Then let's assume we're about to have some company."

Sakev called in to headquarters while I unsnapped my crash webbing and stumbled across a bent and twisted floor to the shuttle's main cabin. It was a total wreck, barely even intact. The sundered armor provided no protection from the icy winds, and I knew it would be even less effective against blaster fire.

We hadn't brought much in the way of weaponry, as we were going on a supply run. We did have an automatic rifle each, with a spare clip for each of us. The only other thing that survived the crash was a service pistol which only held twelve shots, but nothing to reload it with.

"What's it like back there?"

"Not good, but at least we're not completely unarmed. The shuttle is skrell, though."

"Then we can't sit here and play siege. We should get moving."

A thousand little fires of agony spread about my body as I struggled to get back up to the cockpit. I assisted Sakev with disengaging his crash webbing, which had been damaged in the impact. When the buckle wouldn't come unsnapped, I drew my trench knife and cut away at the fabric.

Helping to support Sakev's weight, I got him out of the shuttle and into the snowy jungle. The shuttle's path of descent through the forest was marked by broken tree branches, felled limbs, and sundered metal, some of it still on fire. A blind man could follow such a trail right to us.

"We have to get out of here, find some cover where we can make our stand."

"Too late."

I followed Sakev's pointing finger down the trail of destruction we'd left behind. At first, all I saw were tiny fires and swirling snowflakes. Then I spotted a hooded figure hustling through the sundered jungle limbs. Human, carrying a simple, but nonetheless deadly, rifle.

And he was not alone. I counted at least a dozen more humans coming in his wake, and there were probably more that were obscured by the jungle and the snowfall.

"This is going to be rough."

"Yeah." I flipped the safety off my assault rifle and took cover behind a tree trunk. "For them."

Despite my bravado, I knew we were in deep trouble, and help was likely going to be a long time coming.

SYBIL

"What do you want to tell me?" I asked.

"Why don't you sit back down." My dad patted the floor across from him.

"Are you sure you're okay?" I sat back down and crossed my legs once more.

"I'm great," he smiled and gently touched my knee. "I was going to tell you this when you came back to visit, but I figured I might as well tell you while you're here. I'd hate to inconvenience you."

"You're never an inconvenience, Dad. You know that. I'm only in this city for you."

And maybe Cazak, too.

"You're a sweet kid. Your mother would be so proud."

My apprehension lessened when he brought up mom.

"Is that what you want to talk about?" I asked.

"No," he said. "I want to tell you a story. Do you have time?"

"I have as much time as you need."

"Excellent. It's not a long story, but it's an important one, so I need you to listen very closely."

"Of course, Dad."

"Do you know what the Ancient Ones are? Some of those opposed to us have called us Ancient Enemies. Do you know who they are?" he asked.

"Dottie's mentioned them once or twice, but she hasn't told me anything specific," I replied. His expression lit up.

"Oh, good. The Ancient Ones go by so many names. I'm glad I have the term you know."

Something wasn't right, but I couldn't place it. The way Dottie talked about the Ancient Enemies led me to think that they weren't a good thing. Dad seemed excited to talk about them.

"What are they?" I pressed.

"The Ancient Enemies," he stopped and let out a giggle. "Sorry, it's just a strange name for them compared to all of the others."

"What are their other names?"

"I couldn't even begin to pronounce them," my dad

laughed and shook his head. "One sounds kind of like this." He made a strange gurgling sound that didn't sound like anything.

"I sound pretty crazy trying to pronounce that, right?"

"A little." I laughed nervously.

"The other names aren't important. We can call them the Ancient Enemies for the sake of the story."

"Okay," I nodded. "What are they?"

"They are a race of the most powerful beings in the galaxy. Not just our galaxy, either. Every galaxy."

"Why haven't I seen one before?" I asked.

"A thousand years ago, there was a war. The Ancient Enemies didn't lose, but they did pull back and regroup. It slowed them down for a while, but they were never stopped. Some beings like to think they were stopped, but that's just not true. Can you imagine such arrogance? A lesser species thinking they were powerful enough to permanently stop a race like the Ancient Enemies?"

"It sounds like the Ancient Enemies are the arrogant ones, if you ask me."

Dad considered my statement for a moment.

"I can see why you'd think that," he nodded. "But hopefully, this story will change your way of thinking."

"Can I ask why you're telling me this?" I asked him.

"It's important that you know these things." That

was Dad's go-to answer whenever he wanted to teach me something, even if I never used the knowledge again.

"Dottie said the Ancient Enemies might be what's causing people to act so strange," I said.

"That's somewhat true. I'd argue that the people they touch aren't acting strange, just enlightened."

I felt sick.

"I don't understand," I forced the words out.

"Do you know what a symbiotic relationship is?" Dad asked.

"A mutually beneficial relationship between two species," I rattled off without thinking too much about my words.

"Smart girl!" Dad beamed. "That's exactly right. The Ancient Enemies and humans have a symbiotic relationship. Humans are the perfect hosts for the Ancient Enemies."

My mouth went dry. I was tempted to call the guards but I wanted more information. Maybe Dottie could make heads or tails of this.

"How so?" If my voice sounded strange, Dad didn't notice or comment on it. He kept on with his lesson.

"Humans are overflowing with unchecked ambition. There's not a creature in existence with the same drive as humans."

A few moments ago, Dad had complimented my

drive. I wondered if he was thinking of that talk when he said that.

"Humans are also resilient. They aren't built to survive in a wide range of environments, but does that stop them? No, it doesn't!" Dad was getting excited now. His eyes were wide and bright. He gestured wildly as he talked.

"Once humans decide they want something, they'll go to the ends of the earth to get it," he went on. "Have you ever encountered another species like that? Humans were never meant to be on this planet, yet here they are!"

"Our home planet died, what were we supposed to do?" I asked.

"That right there is exactly what I'm talking about. Most species wouldn't have thought to do anything. The humans sailed into the stars and made a new home for themselves. When they first arrived on this planet, it was the farthest thing from suitable. Sentient plants. Extreme heat. Extreme cold. The humans mastered everything here, or at least figured out how to survive around it. Some of them also managed to fight off the Xathi!"

I shuddered at the name of those horrible aliens. Kaster was spared the brunt of the attack, but that didn't mean it was a safe place during that turbulent time.

"Those Xathi are a piece of work," Dad laughed. "I'd argue that they'd make suitable hosts, as well."

"That doesn't sound like a symbiotic relationship," I pointed out. "The Ancient Enemies take over humans, but what do the humans get out of it?"

"They get to expand their minds. The brightest of the humans seek knowledge with unrivaled hunger. They get a glimpse of all the secrets of the galaxy, every galaxy. They see things no one could ever dream up."

"That's not what's happening," I said. "People are going mad. They're sick. They're in danger."

"Oh, that," Dad waved me off. "The knowledge the humans are exposed to is powerful. Most can't handle having a being such as an Ancient Enemy occupy their minds for longer than a few weeks."

"What happens after a few weeks?" I asked. My stomach churned, despite the fact that I'd skipped breakfast this morning.

"Most humans expire." Dad frowned. The idea of humans dying didn't appear to upset him. He looked more disappointed than anything else. "Some of them are figuring out how to last longer while sharing a mind with an Ancient Enemy."

"How?"

"I don't know yet," he said. "It's no matter. The Ancient Enemies don't get attached to individuals. It's the species that matters. Luckily for them, humans are plentiful and replaceable."

"That's terrible."

"It's the circle of life, darling."

I frowned. Dad's never called me darling, ever.

"It would be against their own survival interest to get attached to one specific human," Dad continued explaining.

"What's the point of this, Dad?" I asked, feeling more uncomfortable by the minute. I didn't like how Dad kept referring to humans as if he was something separate.

"You're my daughter. I love you. I just want you to understand what's happening in the world around you."

"Are you telling me that you know with one hundred percent certainty that the Ancient Enemies are causing the strange behavior of the people contained here?"

"You know what else is remarkable about humans?" Dad breezed by my question.

"What?" I knew I wouldn't like the answer.

"They breed at a remarkable rate. Even if one expires, there's a host of infants."

"Please stop." I closed my eyes and looked away.

"Am I upsetting you?" Dad looked genuinely confused.

"Yes." I got to my feet. "I'm sorry. I have to go."

"I hope you'll come back soon," Dad called after me as I was escorted from the cell. I looked over my shoulder one last time. Dad smiled at me. There was something wrong with that smile. It was just a little too wide for his mouth. I knew at that moment that whatever I'd been talking to for the last hour was not my father.

Pain bloomed in my chest. Would I ever talk to my real dad again? Was he even still in there? Or did an Ancient Enemy take him away from me forever?

CAZAK

Sakev popped around the corner of the tree trunk and unleashed a long burst down range at the anti-alien terrorists. His lips peeled back in a savage snarl, and a scream of rage and determination escaped from behind his teeth.

His aim was true, and one of the charging anti-alienists stopped in his tracks, jerking about as bullets riddled his body. He fell to the snow, bleeding wounds steaming in the cold air.

The rest of the terrorists learned their lesson quickly, and all too well. They stopped trying to charge our position and sought out cover of their own. That was a real shame.

Soon the tree we had sought shelter behind began

taking rounds. The thick trunk provided enough mass to keep the bullets from penetrating to the other side, but the anti-alienists didn't seem to be worried about conserving ammo. Their hail of bullets was so intense they sundered several limbs and caused them to crash to the ground.

I knelt down in the snow and flattened myself against the trunk. Then I shimmied out just enough to get a shot, exposing the bare minimum of my scaled hide for them to target. I flipped the rifle to the semi-automatic setting and sent a controlled burst toward an anti-alienist who had chosen poor cover. He had posted himself up behind a fallen tree, but due to a slight dip in the terrain, his legs were exposed from the knees down.

My burst caught him flush, two in the left knee and one in the right. He screamed, toppling over as his kneecaps became so much splintered bone and steaming, ground meat. Most likely he would bleed out quickly, and even if he didn't, he wouldn't be chasing us anytime soon.

"Nice shot, Cazak."

"Thanks."

I pulled myself back behind the tree trunk when a round came awfully close to hitting me in the neck. Sakev leaned out and fired his own short burst, but he was unable to find a soft target. The barrage from the anti-alien terrorists slowed for a moment while he was firing, but then the return fire forced him to take cover as, well.

For a time, we managed to hold them off by taking turns firing and hiding. We were much better shots, to be sure, but we had to conserve ammunition. By contrast, the terrorists were just firing willy-nilly, but by sheer determination, they had a good chance of hitting us.

Then the bastards got smart, and started anticipating which one of us was going to be firing while the other hid. A barrage tore through the tree trunk, and sent a sharp shard of bark into my face. The gash it left behind wasn't deep, but it did serve to remind us that our time was growing short.

"They're closing in on us. We have to abandon this position."

"You mean retreat?"

"Your leg means that's not an option, or I'd be assholes and elbows right now."

I jerked my head toward a rocky outcropping dusted with snow.

"See that little ridge there?"

"Yeah."

"Count to three, and then move as fast as you can toward it. I'll cover you."

"Are you nuts?"

"Oh, totally. But I've got you. You hear me? I've got you."

Sakev's face fell, and he nodded grimly. We both knew there was a good chance I was about to sell myself to keep him safe, if only for the moment.

But that didn't mean I was about to go down without a fight. I counted to three, drawing my service pistol and wielding the assault rifle in one hand. It's next to impossible to hold it steady enough for anything resembling accuracy with one hand, but I switched it to full auto and hoped for the best.

Scales out, and a guttural growl escaping my lips, I popped out fully from behind the tree wielding both weapons. I didn't even aim, I just sent as many bullets flying as quickly as I could.

To my surprise, I actually took down a terrorist with the assault rifle. The ignorant fellow had been sprinting full tilt toward our position. His bravery cost him a red line of bullet wounds up his torso and across his throat. He fell to the snow, spilling out scarlet atop the blazing whiteness.

The rest of his companions all scrambled to find new cover. A few of them fired back, but in their terror, their shots went wide and I wasn't scratched. The service pistol claimed a victim as I took a man right in the heart. His hand clutched at the rapidly expanding dark spot on his coat before he pitched face first into the snow.

Wisely, I scrambled back behind the tree and used it to block their view as I ran like hell for the ridge. Sakev, hindered by his injured leg, managed to fling himself over it just as I was a dozen paces from safety.

Sakev braced his rifle on the rough stone and laid down some cover fire for me. A scream indicated that he hit someone, but I was in no position to look back and see if it was a killing or disabling shot.

I scrambled over the ridge as bullets ricocheted all around us. When we both started firing, the terrorists dove back into cover, but they had already gained precious ground.

Sakev slammed the spare clip into his rifle and grimaced.

"How many you got left?"

"Less than one fourth of my clip. The pistol's completely out."

"Well, what did you expect, with that kind of gung ho shit?"

"I expected you to die if I didn't empty the clip."

Sakev's eyes grew distant, and then he flipped his rifle into semi-auto mode.

"You have a point. Start running, and I'll keep them

off your back long enough to make your escape. Just tell Evie that I—"

"Shut the fuck up. I'm not leaving you."

"Come on, Cazak, I know you're tough, but what's the point of both of us being killed?"

"We live together, or we die together. We can't stay here, though."

With my back against the ridge, I scoped out a likely new source of cover for us. The only thing I could spot was a thick boled, squat tree. It was nearly fifty feet behind our current position, though.

"You run straight for that twisted-looking tree. I'll angle off to the left and draw their fire."

"That's a skrell plan."

"Go. Get moving."

I shoved Sakev into a stumbling run and popped up from behind the ridge. I let loose a couple of shots to get their attention, and then ran like a madman through the underbrush. Bullets rained all about me, snapping tree limbs and splintering bark from trunks, but somehow, I managed to escape without further injury.

In short order I joined Sakev at our new cover and crouched down in the snow next to him.

"I'm almost out."

"I know. Hang on a minute and I'll see if I can't persuade them to leave us alone."

Sakev leaned out around the trunk, switching his

rifle to single-shot mode. He took a terrorist right between the eyes, the man dead before he even toppled over. Taking careful aim, he sliced right through the exposed thigh of another human. He must have hit the femoral artery, because the man's scream died seconds after he hit the ground as he bled out into the snow.

My companion killed another terrorist, and another, but still they kept coming. Rather than being discouraged by the sight of their dead comrades, they seemed incensed into a frenzy. The fact of the matter was, once they decided to rush us, it would be all over.

"Here." I switched rifles with Sakev. "There's a dense copse not far from us, do you see it?'

"Yeah." Sakev peered behind our position. "I can make it."

"Then go, and don't stop running."

Screaming, I came out from behind the tree and planted my feet wide. At that point, I wanted to terrify the anti-alienists as much as possible. I switched to full auto and sent a deadly hail of bullets at their position.

Men screamed, some even died, but most of my shots fell harmlessly onto tree limbs or jutting stones. A line of gouts in the snow indicated where I'd hit the ground.

Then I was out of ammo, and running like hell for the copse of trees. But when I got there, Sakev just stood there, with his back exposed.

"What the hell, man, keep going—"

I screeched to a halt when I saw what was holding him up. We stood at the edge of a river, its steep rocky banks plunging forty feet before white rapids gushed through the ravine. There was no way to climb, and the water was clearly not deep enough for us to dive.

We looked at each other, knowing we were both dead.

The anti-alienists knew it, too. Sakev emptied the rest of his clip, killing one of their more overzealous members, but then he was empty. They realized we had stopped shooting, and one by one stepped out into the open, many of them grinning sadistically.

I could tell by the hard fires in their eyes that there would be no prisoners taken today. My one regret was not being able to tell Sybil how I really felt...

Then the forest simply came alive. One second, the anti-alien militia was stalking toward us, some already taking aim, and then the green growing things began assaulting them.

Men screamed as vines slithered out and ensnared their limbs. A few fired off utterly ineffectual shots as they were taken captive. Soon, our attackers were splayed out spread eagle as the vines stretched them out like staked rabbit skins.

"The Puppet Master just saved our asses."

"Yeah. We owe our lives to a plant."

We both stared at each other and erupted into laughter which was just one step removed from hysteria. Whether it was because we were glad to be alive, or the utter absurdity of the moment, I still cannot say.

SYBIL

People came and went through the large double doors, but I didn't bother to look up at them. I felt as if I were in a fugue, or a maddening kind of shock, where I couldn't act but still felt each painful jab of my father's words.

The clinical way he'd described humanity still stung me to the core. Ambitious, overzealous. Fast breeders. The perfect hosts to use up and burn through.

Did that mean they were going to 'burn up' my father? Was the alien presence inside his body already killing him? The medical team at the detention center claimed his vitals were all normal. The only signs of any issues were some anomalous readings on his brain scan and EKG.

Others had been possessed by the Ancient Enemies

and still managed to fight them off, and seemed perfectly normal afterward. Cazak had mentioned a friend of a friend, a human named Keith, who had attacked and tried to kill a member of Team Three. Apparently, Keith suffered no long-lasting effects, and was more concerned for the safety of the man he'd attacked than himself.

Then why wouldn't this thing let my father go? Surely it could see that he was no use anymore. He would be kept confined until everyone was absolutely certain the incorporeal possessing entity was gone. So why did it still have its mental meathooks in him?

Those were my thoughts as I struggled to make sense of what my life had become. I felt utterly lost, more lost than if I'd sealed myself in a rocket and launched myself into space with no heading or directional navigation.

Even as I sat there in the detention center lobby, and people flowed in and out, I felt removed from the world. The winter sun beaming cheerfully through the lobby windows did nothing to warm my soul, even though it did heat my skin. Time seemed to have lost its meaning, and the world didn't make any sense.

I had accepted the fact that being the child of a politician meant some hard truths. One of them was that my father was in a potentially hazardous profession. Political leaders are often targets, whether by oppositional groups or just a disgruntled electorate. I'd always held in the back of my mind the possibility that one day I would return home to find my father had met with foul play, or an accident, or just plain succumbed to the stress of his position.

But the nightmare of possession was something I'd never considered, never could have prepared for. Somehow, it was worse than my father being dead. Then I wouldn't have to look at his face, his body, hear his voice as his strings were pulled by some otherworldly entity.

I tried not to give in to despair. I tried to put my faith in the scientists, that they would find some way to free my father from his mental prison, but things seemed bleak. There was just only so much that could be done.

The monster impersonating my father made a big deal of the fact that humans had survived their own extinction. I couldn't help but wonder at the huge, cosmic joke being played on us if we managed to survive on this hostile alien world only to become living meat-suits for evil alien entities.

The sun sank to the horizon, casting the last of its red-gold light over the city. I wondered if the sun would soon set upon my father, as well.

At last, I could not stand it any longer. I felt as if I would be sucked down into the chasm of my own despair, if I hadn't already. I longed for Cazak, to feel his touch again. As silly as it may seem, I just wanted someone to hold me and tell me everything would be all right, even if we had no way of truly knowing that.

I rose suddenly, startling the clerks behind the desk. At that point, I believed I'd been sitting there so long they had begun to consider me part of the furniture. I swaddled myself in my long coat and headed out into the chill air.

Where would Cazak be at that time of day? He was on duty, and I'd remembered seeing his cousin Jalok on guard duty at the airfield. I headed off that way at a brisk pace, hoping that soon I would feel his gentle touch on my skin.

I don't know why, but as soon as I rounded the corner and the airfield came into view, I felt a creeping sense of trepidation. With no evidence to support my prophecy, I believed something was amiss. The human guards at the gate acted stiff and formal, refusing me entrance until I mentioned that I was the mayor's daughter. Then they grew most cooperative, falling all over each other in a sycophantic way to please me.

I just wanted the gate opened. As soon as it had parted half a foot, I squeezed myself through and took off at a near run toward the tarmac.

Team Three's usual shuttle came into view, and at first, I didn't see anyone. Then Jalok struggled down the ramp holding an enormous piece of equipment. He settled it onto the ground and wiped his brow before he noticed my approach.

"Sybil?" He looked me up and down, his gaze settling on my face. One look at my expression and he knew I was upset. "What's wrong? What are you doing here?'

"I—I really need to speak with Cazak. Is he here?"

His brow furrowed in confusion.

"No, he has duties elsewhere. I'm not sure what."

I tried to keep the frustration out of my tone when I spoke again.

"Can you try to find out? I'm sorry, but something's —something's happened and I really need to see him."

"Ah, alright." Jalok turned around and dug out his comms unit. I shifted nervously from foot to foot while he made the call.

"Hey, Navat, you know where Cazak is on duty today? Oh yeah, a supply run to Amarita? Man, wish I could get the cushy details. Do you have any idea when he's coming back?"

Jalok turned his face away from the comm.

"He's checking right now."

"Thank you."

I heard a distorted voice on the comm. Jalok listened intently, his face falling into a worried frown.

"We're mobilizing now? All right, let me get this

heap in the air and I'll come pick you up."

Jalok started up the ramp, stopping at the last minute as if he'd just remembered I was there.

"Cazak and Sakev's shuttle went down."

"Went down? You mean *crashed?*"

Jalok nodded grimly.

"Early reports are blaming the anti-alien separatists. We just picked up their distress signal and are heading that way to help. You should, uh, sit down or something, alright?"

Then he darted up the ramp and I stared in shock as the shuttle lifted off the ground.

Cazak's shuttle had gone down.

Anti-alienists shot him down.

Cazak was gone.

My life had become a living nightmare.

Numb to the chill wind, or the way it blew my hair into total disarray, I stumbled down the tarmac and out the gate. The guards exchanged glances as I passed, but offered no assistance. As if they could have helped me anyway.

No one could help me. My father was held prisoner, both physically at the detention center and mentally by the Ancient Enemy hiding in his brain. The one person who could have, maybe, helped me deal with it had been shot down. Shot down. Just because a distress beacon was being sent didn't mean he was still alive.

With no real direction or goal, I wandered through the city streets. My nose grew cold, then lost feeling, and I didn't care. At some point, my body overrode my mind and I wound up heading inside Dottie's apartment complex.

No one paid me any attention as I slunk into a corner, held my head in my hands, and sobbed. My shoulders shook, wracked with spasm after spasm, and my throat grew raw, but I still continued to cry. I had never felt so completely hopeless in my entire life.

Then I felt hands on my shoulders, shaking me, picking me up and embracing me. Dottie and Evie were there, holding me tight. I clung to them like a swimmer clings to a rock in a stormy sea.

"It's all right, honey." Dottie stroked my hair as she spoke. "It's going to be okay."

"Cazak's a fighter, and tough as they come." Evie sounded as if she were trying to convince herself as much as me. "And Sakev knows I'll never forgive him if he gets killed. They're going to make it."

"They're working round the clock to figure out a way to cure your father, too." Dottie's voice was brimming with conviction, but I noticed that she didn't say they would cure him, just that they were trying.

Such cold comfort was all I really had, but Dottie and Evie made it easier to bear.

Some.

CAZAK

Sakev and I leaned our backs against the rough bark of a tree while we watched the anti-alienists squirm in their vine cocoons. If it hadn't been for the Puppet Master's intervention, we would have been toast.

We joked for a time about how many of the anti-alienists had dark spots on the fronts of their pants. We weren't in a mood for sympathy, not in the slightest.

They'd shot us down, after all, and then tried to kill us.

That kinda dampened any friendly feeling.

I suppose we should have been worried about the political ramifications of what had happened, but honestly, we were just glad to have come out relatively unscathed. It had been a nasty, brutal firefight, but we'd won, along with some help from our generous benefactor, the Puppet Master.

Part of me wished the Puppet Master would just send vines up to strangle each and every one of the damn anti-alienists, but that was both wishful thinking and short-sighted on my part. After all, killing the anti-alienists would just confirm that their prejudices were right all along. Normally, I wouldn't care so much about stuff like that, but after having gotten involved with Sybil Anatosian, my perspective on many things had changed drastically. I was now playing the long game, rather than just trying to get through my next duty assignment or bottle of booze.

I suppose that's why I'd fought so damn hard against the anti-alien terrorists. I had something to fight for now, maybe for the first time in a long time.

The sound of engines stirred us from our conversation. I looked up into the sky and saw an extra-large shuttle descending from the skies amid the swirling flurries. Sakev and I exchanged glances, because brass didn't usually send out such a fuel-inefficient vehicle.

"Damn, I guess we rate luxury."

"No, it's probably just so that they have room for all the prisoners."

Sakev looked over at the struggling, despairing

bodies writhing in the constricting vines of the Puppet Master.

"Yeah, you're probably right."

The shuttle came down, blasting us with a hot breeze from its engine that actually felt quite nice under the circumstances. A ramp descended from the rear, and the first one down the pike was none other than Sk'lar. He was wielding one of those monster assault rifles that usually only the Valorni were strong enough to use properly. His black eyes were narrowed to slits, and he cast about in search of a target that was not forthcoming.

He was quickly followed by Navat, Tyehn, Jalok, and —to our surprise—the entirety of teams one and two.

"We merit some consideration, with three strike teams."

"Yeah, I guess they love us, after all."

Sk'lar strode up to us, a ghost of a smile flitting across his dour face for just an instant, the only sign I was likely to get that he was glad I was still alive.

"Cazak, report."

I opened my mouth to speak, but Jalok shoved into the front of the pack and glared at Sk'lar.

"Report? Are you out of your mind? Can't you see these guys are exhausted?"

"I'm fine, cousin. Sakev is healed, too." I flashed him a smile to show that I appreciated his rancor on my behalf, and then turned to address my commander. "There's not a lot to tell. Sakev and I were flying back after our supply drop when we encountered artillery fire. Big enough to bring down our shuttle. From there, we engaged the enemy until the Puppet Master decided to give us some much needed backup."

Sk'lar nodded, likely having inferred that much from the struggling forms of the anti-alienists.

"Looks like a catch of the day." Jalok cackled at the furious human captives. "Not so damn smug now, are you? Let's hear some of those anti-alien slogans come out of your mouths now."

"Jalok, don't taunt the prisoners. It's unprofessional."

"Very well, sir." Jalok's salute turned into an obscene gesture when Sk'lar turned back to face Sakev and me.

"You men did good work here today. I'll be sure to put a commendation on your report."

"Did you hear that?" Sakev turned a grin toward me. "He wants to give us a condemnation."

"Better to be damned for what we are, right?"

Sk'lar actually smiled for a moment.

"You two can go inside the shuttle where it's warm. The rest of us will handle the cleanup."

"Music to my ears, Commander."

"Finally, you say something that actually makes sense, Sk'lar."

We headed up the ramp, gratefully sighing as the warmth of the shuttle's cabin enveloped our tired muscles. Outside, I heard Sk'lar bark at Jalok to tend to our wounds. While he was patching us up, Jalok filled us in on what had happened while we were away.

"So, Dottie got an alert informing Sybil that her father wanted to see her."

"How's he doing?"

Jalok frowned, pausing in his ministrations for just a moment.

"Physically, he's doing fine. Do you want to hear this or are you going to keep interrupting me?"

"I want to hear it, I want to hear it. Go on."

"Right. So Sybil got called in to see her father, and at first, everything seemed just fine. He was engaging, cheerful, and to all appearances, he seemed to be back to his old self. They were just about to set him loose, too, when all of a sudden, he says he has something important to say to his daughter."

Sakev and I leaned forward, eager to hear the next bit.

"So then he starts talking real crazy and skrell. Like, he called the Ancient Enemies glorious or something like that."

"No!"

"Unfortunately, yes. He went on and on about how

powerful and great they were, and get this; apparently humans are the perfect hosts for them."

That made my skin crawl, because I realized that Sybil was going to be in great danger just by being one of her species.

"Perfect hosts?"

"Yeah, I guess they're compatible. He also said humans were the most resilient beings in the galaxy or some shit. That was why they were the perfect hosts, too."

"How did Sybil take it?"

"How do you think she took it? She's devastated."

"I have to get back to her. When do we take off?"

"Slow down, cousin. I know you're eager, but we have a lot of cleanup to take care of here first. You're relieved of duty for the time being."

"Can you do that? You're not Sk'lar—"

"Shut up and take it easy. Or I'll cut off your other ear."

A few days ago, that would have really pissed me off. But now that I knew it wasn't an issue for Sybil, I was free to laugh along with him.

It took a couple of hours for them to finally get everything cleaned up at the battle site.

There were prisoners to secure, once we convinced the Puppet Master to let them go, and quite a few bodies to be attended to.

Sk'lar then ordered a full recon of the area, just in case there were more of the anti-alienists lurking in the woods, or maybe even a base camp, but they came up emptyhanded.

Finally, finally, we took off from the crash site and headed for Nyheim.

I spent the whole time wondering what I was going to say to Sybil. What can you say to someone whose only parent's mind has been controlled by an evil, ancient alien force? Somehow, 'I'm sorry' didn't seem like it would be sufficient.

The shuttle landed and, as soon as the ramp hit the tarmac, I was bugging out. I ran nearly all the way from the airfield to Dottie's place, and then knocked on the door. Sybil answered it and we stood there for a minute staring at each other.

Then we surged forward and clutched each other in a fierce, passionate embrace. During the battle with the anti-alienists, I'd felt certain I wouldn't live to hold her in my arms again. So I wasn't going to miss that opportunity for the world.

At length, we headed inside, holding hands, and sat down on the sofa. I wasn't sure where Dottie had gotten off to, but we had the place to ourselves.

"I missed you."

Sybil put her hand on top of my own and squeezed tightly.

"I missed you, too."

"I'm sorry about your father. I wish there was something I could do."

"I know. It's hard, but I'll keep on going. What else can I do? I'm sorry you were almost killed."

I shrugged.

"Goes with the territory of being a soldier." I sighed and put my hand on her smooth cheek. "Listen, Sybil. When I was fighting for my life out there, the worst thought that I had was that I would never see you again. So I swore that if I got the chance, I'd tell you how I feel. I know this is all new, and big, and overwhelming, but I think I'm falling in love with you."

Sybil clapped a hand over her mouth and a strangled sob escaped her throat. For a moment I thought I'd gone too far, but then she clutched me and cried into my chest.

"Cazak, I'm falling in love with you, too. I can't even imagine my life without you in it now. I hope that you never leave me."

I suppose I must have got some debris in my eyes during the firefight, because there were tears streaming down my cheeks, as well. I swept her up into my arms and carried her off to the bedroom. But I closed the door behind us, because love, like fighting, should never have a witness.

SYBIL

I spent a long, sleepless night at Dottie's place, staring at the ceiling and trying not to think about my father. I'd barely slept a wink the night before. My mind kept dwelling on the awfulness of what had happened to him.

If I hadn't been reeling from my father's possession under the influence of an otherworldly entity, I would have had more time to freak out over what had happened to Cazak and Sakev. The anti-alienists had been agitating for some time, teasing and sometimes inciting violence, but never a blatant attack. And against a military craft, bound on a humanitarian mission delivering food. It beggared the imagination that they would have the gall.

For two days, I tried to sort things out in my head,

but came no closer to anything resembling clarity. The only thing I could really be sure of is how I felt about Cazak. Strong, smart, funny, but with an edge, my love for him was something I could cling to amid the tempest that my life had become.

I also knew that I was terrified of being possessed as my father had been. Every time I felt like drifting to sleep, paranoia would strike and I'd wonder if I were truly about to slumber or if I were in fact falling under the spell of one of those monsters.

The small hours of the morning passed, and the weak winter sun cast its ghostly light, thinned by light overcast, through the tiny bedroom window. I didn't move, unable to sleep, even though I was tired, and watched the shadows grow longer.

When they had stretched halfway across the room, I stood up at last and headed into the bathroom. After a quick bath, I brushed out my hair, put on some cosmetics, and dressed myself nicely, as if I would be appearing at an official social function.

I added a diamond pendant which my father had bought for me on one of my birthdays. It was a bit gaudy and ostentatious, but my father loved it and I hoped that if there were some shred of him left inside the husk in that cell, that it might stir his memory.

Though I could have called a car, I decided to walk to the detention center instead. Perhaps I was giving myself time to steel my nerve, or perhaps I just wanted to delay the misery of seeing him in such a pathetic state. The chill winter wind cut through even my thick coat like a knife, but it didn't hold a candle to the cold despair numbing my heart.

Once I reached the detention center, I had to wait in the lobby while I was cleared to see my father again. I tried to press the guard for information, but he remained tight-lipped. Part of me was hoping beyond hope that my father would be back to normal already, an overnight miracle which answered the hopes and prayers of my inner child.

Soon, I was shown into the hallway outside his cell. One look at my father and I knew that he was still under the thrall of the Ancient Enemy. A thin smile stretched over his stolen face, but his eyes remained cold and distant.

"Hello, offspring."

"Don't call me that." I crossed my arms over my chest. "I want to talk to my father, not to you."

The smile remained intact. I flinched when the thing masquerading as my father suddenly stood up and walked to the middle of the cell.

"I'm afraid that will be quite impossible. This is my body now, until I see fit to discard it for another."

I suppressed a shudder at the sound of the word

'discard'. Ignoring what it had said, I stared into my father's blank gaze.

"Daddy, are you in there? Answer me, please. You have to fight this thing and come back to me."

The thing wearing my father shook his head.

"You do not understand, offspring. It is your belief that being a vessel for a superior being is some sort of malignancy, like a disease, rather than a rare opportunity to touch the hem of greatness."

I pounded my fist against the bars of his cell, too angry and frustrated to notice the pain.

"Daddy, come on, talk to me. You can beat this thing, you're stronger than it is."

The Ancient Enemy's only response was to take another step toward the bars. It was now within arm's length, and could reach out to seize me through the bars, but I was too distraught to care.

In desperation, I lifted up the pendant around my neck and held it out like an offering.

"Look, you remember this necklace, don't you, Daddy? You gave it to me on my birthday."

My father's face was crossed by what may have been interest. He walked forward and reached out to stroke the pendant.

"This necklace..."

"Yes, Daddy? Do you remember now?"

"It's constructed of pressurized carbon and soft,

weak metal. Such baubles will be obsolete in the new Galactic order."

"Damn it." I hung my head in utter misery. "Why can't you just let him go? First, my father gets possessed, and then anti-alienists shoot down Cazak's shuttle, and--"

"Pardon me, did you say that Cazak's shuttle was attacked?"

I paused, unsure if I should continue, but my vague hope of freeing my father overrode any desire not to spill sensitive information to an enemy.

"Yes, anti-alienists shot them down on their way back from a supply run. Cazak and Sakev were nearly killed, and a lot of the anti-alienists died."

"Intriguing. And most useful."

My father—no, not my father, the thing wearing his skin—had heard of how two good men had nearly been killed, and he thought it was intriguing. I was truly disgusted by what had been done to him.

"Thank you for this information, offspring. I want you to know that we are not heartless beings. I am sorry for the pain I am about to cause you."

"Pain?" I stepped away from the bars, fearing the worst. Could my father, under the Ancient Enemy's control, tear right through the bars of his cell?

My father's mouth opened so wide I could see his molars. He let out a scream which would have been more appropriate in a jungle or zoo than coming out of a man's mouth. Later, I would realize it was the same type of scream the newly possessed made.

He dashed across the cell toward the concrete wall. At the last moment, he ducked his head and a sickening thud made me cover my mouth in horror.

My father fell backward, his forehead bleeding into his left eye. But he didn't blink, and the white of his eye soon turned crimson with the constant flow of blood. Another scream ripped from his mouth, and he charged at the opposite side of his cell.

"Father, stop! You're killing yourself."

I couldn't watch as he slammed into the wall again.

The room was monitored and as security guards rushed to the door, I hoped that they'd stop him.

But it didn't work. The door was jammed from the inside with something alien I couldn't make out.

I closed my eyes. When I opened my eyes, there were two matching bloodstains on opposite sides of the cell. Groggily, my father rose to his feet and swayed a moment before taking aim at the iron bars which separated us.

"No, don't make him do this, please." I had changed my appeal to the one in control of the moment, which was the Ancient Enemy. "Stop. Please don't hurt him anymore."

The alien entity screamed, and charged for the bars.

The resounding impact rang in my ears for what felt like an eternity. My father fell to the concrete floor, bleeding badly. He lifted his head with difficulty, and one of his eyeballs dangled from the socket by a strand of bloody tissue.

"Oh my god." I covered my mouth with both hands. I wanted to vomit, I wanted to scream, I wanted to run away, but all I could do was watch as my father's body was pushed back to its feet by the monster in the driver's seat.

He screamed again, a guttural, horrid sound, and half-ran, half-stumbled across the cell toward the first bloodstain he had made. My eyes remained transfixed in utter, gruesome fascination as his head crashed into the unyielding concrete. That time, that final time, there was a wet sound, akin to a ripe melon being dropped on the floor.

My father fell backward onto the cold concrete, his forehead caved in. The bloody mask that used to be his face made me scream until my throat was raw.

Dead. My father was dead. And I had watched him be murdered right before my eyes.

CAZAK

I shifted uncomfortably in my seat at the council table, hemmed in on all sides by bigwigs. I felt like a teeny tiny fish in a gigantic ocean.

I knew Sybil had been planning to visit her father that day, but I couldn't miss this.

No one could.

General Rouhr was in charge of the proceedings. The severe military commander had an uncharacteristically worried frown adorning his already dour face. Given the topic of conversation, I didn't blame him one bit.

Fen, Evie, Dottie, and the rest of the science crew were part of the proceedings, as well. The science types seemed less worried than the rest of us, more focused on their tasks. I guess it goes with being a scientist.

They were looking at the Ancient Enemies as a problem to be solved, rather than a terrifying force which could seize control of any of them at the drop of a hat.

Most of the strike teams were present as well, including our leadership. Sk'lar had an inscrutable, blank expression on his ebony face. But then again, my commander always was hard to read, so he could have been panicking on the inside for all I knew. You'd never have known from his poise, though.

Cousin Jalok was on duty, so I didn't see him in the chamber, but Sakev was there. Our recent experience with the anti-alienist movement seemed to make us expert witnesses, or something.

You couldn't turn around without running into somebody important in that room. In short, it was the last place I wanted to be, other than a battlefield.

The room buzzed with low conversations, most of them focused on the Ancient Enemies, but more than a few sounded personal. It seemed like many of the people in that chamber knew someone, even if only by proxy, who had suffered a possession-type event.

At length, General Rouhr rose to his feet and tapped his metal drinking vessel on the table. The conversations died down to a total hush quickly, but he waited patiently while everyone settled in and turned their attention toward him.

"I'm certain that many of you know that this meeting was called so we could disseminate information about our new, daunting foes, the Ancient Enemies. We've made something of a break-through, thanks to the efforts of Fen and the Puppet Master."

It was at that point that I realized there was another presence in the chamber, even if it was only mental. The Puppet Master's consciousness was focused on that room, and once I picked up on his telepathic presence, I was unsure as to why I hadn't noticed it before.

General Rouhr turned his gaze on Fen.

"Doctor, if you'd care to take the floor?"

Fen stood up and took us all in with her gaze. As a Urai, she'd always been inscrutable, but her eyes burned with a cold passion that made me especially uncomfortable on that day.

"For months we've been plagued by enemies which we cannot see, or touch, or smell, or sense in any tangible way. These incorporeal beings have wormed their way into our midst without triggering any alarms, or providing the slightest clues as to their motivations. I'm sure many of you know someone who was possessed by these mysterious and enigmatic life forms."

Her digital voice seemed ominous as it emanated from her box, even though it had the same calm tone as ever.

A lot of nods went around the table, including my own. I couldn't help but feel a stab of sympathy for what Sybil was going through with her father. I hoped that they were able to treat him at the detention center and figure out a way to return him to normal.

"We've been referring to these strange creatures as the Ancient Enemies, because that's what the Puppet Master's species called them. However, while working together with our erstwhile host, I managed to find the true origins of our foes, and their true names."

Gasps went around the council chamber. General Rouhr didn't seem to be surprised, so I figured he'd been updated on that information already. He banged his vessel on the table a few more times until the room grew silent.

Once it was quiet, Fen continued her oration.

"We believe that the Ancient Enemies were once a race called the Gorgoxians."

She fiddled with her datapad, and a holographic display came up in the center of the table. The Gorgoxians seemed much like any other sapient race we'd encountered, with two locomotion limbs and two for manipulation of their environment. Of the various species occupying the council chamber, they most resembled humans.

"These Gorgoxians were very scientifically advanced, light years ahead of their closest neighbors.

According to our research, they had solved many of their society's problems except for one. They had no answer for the eventual expiration of their physical bodies."

I took a drink of water from my own vessel and swallowed hard. I didn't like the implications of what she was saying, not one bit.

"That's right. The Gorgoxians decided to do their level best and cheat death itself. They found a way—we are unsure of how they managed it, exactly—but the Gorgoxians managed to shed their physical forms and became incorporeal beings of pure energy."

That jibed with everything we'd learned so far. I was wondering when they were going to get to the good part, though.

How were we going to kill them?

Fen continued with her lecture after the chamber calmed down once again.

"It gets worse, I'm afraid. It turns out that we've been fighting the Gorgoxians all along, albeit by proxy."

She changed the settings on her datapad, and the image of the Gorgoxian disappeared, replaced with the insectoid form we were all too familiar with, the Xathi.

"It would seem that once the Gorgoxians had shed their physical forms, they were unable to directly interact with the physical world. They solved that problem by taking over the bodies of corporeal creatures. We believe it was their influence that led the Urai to create the Xathi in the first place. They manipulated races to breed disorder and chaos."

Angry, agitated comments rolled through the chamber. Rouhr had to bang his cup several times in an increasingly forceful manner to get silence.

"What's more," Fen continued, "the Gorgoxians were the ones who taught the Urai how to use rift technology. When we began to use it, we awoke the Gorgoxians from whatever torpor they had fallen into, and brought them on us."

Sk'lar and I exchanged glances. The rifts had been extremely useful, and then, all of a sudden, Fen had refused to allow any of us to actually use them. Now we understood why.

I wondered if the Gorgoxians had had anything to do with Tyehn and Maki winding up in the Puppet Master's main antechamber when they attempted to rift out of the jungle. I only succeeded in making my head hurt. I'm no scientist.

"We can only guess at the Gorgoxian's intentions, but all of our guesses seem to indicate they are hostile. If they are taking over humans, which they claim make fabulous hosts, then we are on the precipice of a new war, a war which will make the battle against the Xathi seem like a schoolyard scuffle."

The chamber erupted into questions. It took Fen

several moments to get some semblance of order so she could begin to answer them.

"Yes, Commander Sk'lar?"

Sk'lar stood up and straightened his uniform.

"Fen, have you come up with any countermeasures we can use to guard against possession?"

Fen shook her head.

"No, we have not." She indicated another member of the council, Daxion. The crossbow-wielding warrior didn't bother to stand up to ask his query.

"Fen, do we have any avenue of attack against the Ancient—I mean, the Gorgoxians?"

Fen's expression didn't change when she spoke again.

"No. We do not."

That set the chamber into a near panic. Everyone was talking at once, until General Rouhr grew frustrated and declared the meeting at an end.

Many of the beings in the chamber began to filter out, still agitated. I suspected that even though the meeting was supposed to be classified, the news would quickly spread across the colony.

I rose from my seat and started working my way through the throng toward the exit. General Rouhr bent low to take a call at his console, and his face fell as if someone had just walked over his grave.

"Wait, Cazak." He summoned me over with a furtive gesture.

"Yes, General?"

He looked at me grimly for a moment before speaking again.

"I need you to head to the detention center right away. There's been a—a development."

My blood ran cold, because the first thought in my mind was that Sybil had been injured or possessed.

"What kind of development?"

If the general picked up on the panic in my voice, he gave no sign.

"It's Mayor Anatosian. He's dead."

I took off out of the chamber at a dead run. Sybil. My poor Sybil.

SYBIL

Someone was holding me.

I looked up to see Cazak's orange face looking down at me and his eyes looked as if he had been crying.

Why was he crying?

It wasn't his father that had been taken over and killed by some being that no one knew anything about.

Everything felt distant, wrapped in cotton.

It wasn't his father that had bounced his skull off the side of the cell so many times that it broke open and spilled blood and brains onto his face and onto the floor.

Oh my god, my father was dead.

I didn't bother to hold it back anymore. I just let the sobs rack my body and I cried into Cazak's chest.

I didn't know how long I'd cried for and I no longer cared. I didn't care about anything anymore. There was no point.

There was nothing left for me, except memories.

Like the ones I had of my mother. She was a beautiful woman, full of life and nothing but smiles. Even when she was mad and disappointed, she always found a way to smile. She'd probably find a way to smile at this, as well. She'd probably say something like, "Baby, keep your head up. Your father wouldn't want you to dwell on the final moments when his mind and body were not his own. You need to focus on the good things, the happy memories. Do you remember that one time camping out by the waterfall?"

Of course, I did remember the waterfall. It was one of the happiest moments our family had had. It was also the last happy memory we had before my mother was diagnosed with a disease we determined recently to be called NOX. NOX, that genetic disease that ended up killing everyone afflicted with it before, or shortly after, they turned fifty.

Mother was fifty-one.

I didn't have it, though. It may have been genetic, but apparently it could skip a generation. She had gotten it from her mother, but so far, I'd been spared.

I was given a clean health report as recently as three months ago, but I'd always go in for tests.

The waterfall trip had been fun. Dad had set aside everything business and political to spend an entire week camping with us. And he was *terrible* at it, but we didn't tell him that. The fact that he had been trying so hard to camp, to look like he knew what he was doing, and to look like he was happy, we didn't want to mess that up. And, he was happy.

We all were. We spent an entire week at that waterfall that we had found by accident. Instead of making the turn that we always made to go to the small lake in the mountains like we did every year, Dad had missed the turn, swearing that he hadn't. Then we'd ended up finding the waterfall, and everything was perfect.

It wasn't a big one, maybe ten or twelve feet tall, but it was fed by an amazingly clear stream that dropped into a beautiful pool of water that was so insanely clear and cold, that it was impossible to stay out of it. We had, after bravely getting ourselves used to the temperature of the water, spent the first day swimming and playing together.

I was fourteen at the time.

I had been growing into the role of a teenager, the one that didn't want her parents around. The one that was petulant and mean because her friends were that way. The one where fashion and material things were more important than taking care of the people around you.

But that week at the waterfall, all of that meant nothing. All of that was gone as I spent time with my parents and hurt myself laughing. We weren't a successfully rich family, we were just a family. We weren't politically oriented, we were family oriented.

The third night there was etched into my memory. We had gone hiking earlier in the day, found a small pond full of fish and fished, then went back to the waterfall to cook them and eat them. We had gotten up at first light and had a nice breakfast. Then, while we were hiking, my mom and dad were holding hands and smiling at each other.

That was something they hadn't done outside of the house in years, thanks to my dad's public persona. They were happy, and I was happy. I didn't have a care in the world and I wasn't a teenager anymore, I was a little girl with her parents.

I laughed when dad broke his fishing pole. He had cast out the line, gotten it stuck somehow, and in a little fit of frustration, yanked on it and snapped the thing. The look on his face when his super expensive, unbreakable fishing pole broke, my mom and I laughed until we were in tears, and I still laughed. I'd laughed so hard, I'd pulled a muscle in my ribs. I spent the next few days groaning in pain whenever I laughed or took a deep breath.

But it had been worth it. That look on his face had been so priceless. He did better with my spare pole. We ended up fishing for hours and had a competition on who could catch more fish, me or him. Poor mom, she tried so hard, but she only caught one fish, never able to set the hook right.

It came down to me and dad, and he cheated. I had the fish on the line, everything was set and I was reeling it in, then, when dad grabbed the net to help get the fish out of the water, he "slipped" and dropped the net, letting my fish go. He caught one more before we left, giving him the nine-to-eight win.

He'd cheated. Not that I'd cared, really. We had fun and we were acting like a family.

Then, three days after we got home from the trip, mom got sick and we rushed her to the hospital. That's when we found out about the NOX. That's when dad stopped smiling and got really serious. He had me tested so many times, the doctors said I was anemic.

Seven years later, four hundred tests later, only a few dozen times smiling together as a family, and mother was in the hospital, dying. My last memory of my mother was seeing her connected to machines with dozens of tubes that were monitoring her, helping her breathe, and beeping in rhythm to her heartbeat.

Daddy didn't want me to see her that way, so he led me out of the room. She was gone a few minutes later.

Just like dad was now. Both of my parents taken by something I couldn't see. Both of my parents killed in front of me by something I couldn't see, something I couldn't understand, something that I couldn't fathom. And all I wanted was to get away from it all.

I looked up at Cazak. "Can you get me out of here?"

"Are you sure?" he asked, his voice a little husky. I wasn't sure how long I had cried or sat in his arms remembering my mother or the last time my father and I laughed together, real, joyful laughter, but it must have been quite a bit of time. His eyes looked as if he had been dozing off. Then again, maybe he had just been trying to stay quiet for me.

I nodded. "Yes. I don't want to be here anymore. My father's body is in another room not far from here and I don't want to be around that. I need to get out of here, and if you don't want to take me, I'll go myself."

"No, no. I'll take you. Where do you want to go?"

"I don't care. Just not here." I really didn't care, and I didn't know anyone here. Well, that was a lie, I knew Dottie who lived here now, and Cazak, who apparently lived here with the rest of the *Vengeance* crew. But I didn't know where they lived.

"Well, I can either take you to my place or to

Dottie's. My place is very, utilitarian, from what I've been told. Dottie's is a little more comfortable," he said.

"Fine, whatever. Dottie's is fine. I just want to get out of here. Please."

He nodded and helped me to my feet.

He led me out of the break room and we were in a hallway. "Um, I'm sorry, but the only way out is past the cells."

Past the room where my father had killed himself, or had been forced to kill himself by whatever had possessed him. I nodded and he took my hand and helped lead me past the cells. I didn't want to, but I looked. His body was gone, but the blood was still inside, on the walls and on the door.

A shudder ran through my body and Cazak pulled me a little faster out of the building. Snow was falling as he led me to Dottie's and away from my dead father.

CAZAK

As I worked in Dottie's kitchen preparing a snack for Sybil, I was struck by the fact that, for the first time in my life, I felt truly helpless.

There were many times during my military career where things got dicey, and I knew in my heart there was a possibility that I might lose my life. But in those situations, I still retained some measure of control.

If I were smart enough, fast enough, and lucky enough, if I made the jump to cover or I hit my wild one-in-a-hundred shot, then I could still make it out alive. Even when Sakev and I had been trapped on the steep banks of that rushing river in the jungle, with the terrorists closing in, there had been a measure of control. We could have pleaded for our lives, or chosen to end them by jumping into the river. Or we could have drawn our trench knives and attempted to sell ourselves as dearly as possible.

But as Sybil, the woman I cared for more deeply than anyone else in the galaxy, sat in Dottie's living space and wept softly, I knew for the first time what it meant to be truly helpless. What could I possibly have done in that situation which would make the slightest difference?

Mayor Anatosian was dead. He—no, the thing inside him, the thing controlling him, the Gorgoxian—had smashed his own head against the walls of his cell again and again.

Right in front of Sybil. She had to watch while that thing, that inhuman monster, murdered her father. I suppose she also knew what it was to be completely, totally helpless in the face of tragedy.

All I could do for her on that most terrible of days was be present. I couldn't change what had happened, or protect her from the profound sense of grief and loss which enveloped her soul. What I could do was provide the proverbial shoulder to cry on. I'd performed that task many times already since our reunion, and I was prepared to do it all night if I had to.

I prepared a plate of cheese, root spices, and a hearty but flavorful bread, my slices meticulous and precise. My mind was overwhelmed with all of the craziness that had happened, and the simple task helped keep me from basically losing my mind.

To be honest, the Xathi scared me. I had never let the fear override my duties, or let it control me, but they were terrible foes and utterly without pity. But just as I once thought I knew what helplessness was, I had also realized that I only thought I knew what fear was.

Fear of death is something that every soldier has to accept, and overcome. Only fools have no fear, despite whatever macho rhetoric you might hear us banter about. Every one of us is scared of dying every time we head into battle. Sk'lar likes to read human philosophy, because of course he does, but one line had always stuck with me.

If you head into battle focused on staying alive, you will die. But if you stay focused on winning, you will live. Or something like that. The real version was grimmer, I think.

On that day, however, I found that fear of death paled in comparison to the fear of what the Gorgoxians represented. The Xathi, as horrifying as they were, could be fought. Strategies could be formed and executed against them.

The Gorgoxians, or Ancient Enemies, or whatever one wanted to call them, were far more insidious. As far as we knew, they could take over any human at any time they wanted, with very little to help discern the difference. That meant that Sybil, my beloved Sybil, could be taken over at any time, as well.

My mind raced with utter, sheer nightmare scenarios. What was to stop the Ancient Enemies from taking over Sybil? Or any of the friends or loved ones we had?

I focused on my task, and it helped a little. When I returned to the living space, Sybil had finished her latest crying fit, and was wiping her face with a damp wash cloth. She gave me a sad smile when I laid the platter in front of her.

"You're so kind, but I can't eat right now."

"You haven't eaten all day. Please, try a little."

She picked up a wedge of cheese and nibbled on it. I poured her a small glass of liquor because I figured she needed it, and she made that disappear. Once the alcohol loosened her up a bit and put a fog on her grief, she ate with a bit more enthusiasm, though I could tell she was still in misery.

"Sybil, I needed to say something to you."

She looked up at me with those gorgeous brown eyes, and I nearly lost my nerve. Not for the first time, I wondered how something so beautiful could ever be involved with a scarred grunt like me.

"What is it?"

"I want you to know, that no matter what happens, I'm going to be there for you. I'll do my best to protect you, no matter what, and even if I can't always save the day, I'll be there for you when you need me."

She sniffled a bit and leaned against my chest. Her long hair tickled the side of my cheek as Sybil nuzzled up against me.

"You're the only thing in my life that's gone right in a long time." My heart started beating faster, which I am sure she could feel with her head on my chest. "I feel safe in your arms."

Sybil lifted her head to lock gazes with me. There was still sadness, but there was hope, as well. I leaned in and she matched me, and we gently kissed.

I pulled away from her and put my hand on her cheek, but she moved back in, eager for more. Our kisses grew more intimate, more insistent. Little sighs and gasps escaped both of our mouths as we tasted each other.

"Please make love to me," she breathed into my ear. "Please. I want to forget everything."

"Sybil," I replied. "You need to face your pain."

"Right now, I only want to feel loved and safe, Cazak," she pleaded.

"I don't want to be just a distraction to you," I couldn't help but say.

"You're not," she said, steadying herself and looking at me. "You're my rock."

I saw she was telling the truth.

That she loved me. As I loved her.

My tongue invaded her ready mouth as I held the back of her head, and my other hand slid down her sinuous spine. Sybil's hands tugged at my outer shirt, fumbling with the snaps as we both began to give in to our baser instincts.

I pulled the shoulder straps on her dress down to her elbows, exposing the perfection of her heavy round breasts. Sybil jerked my shirt open and ran her nails across my chest. Her half-closed eyes blazed with desire, and just the sight of her half naked caused my member to stiffen into rock hardness.

"What's this?" Her husky whisper contained a note of teasing mischief. I moaned as Sybil ground her crotch against the straining erection which was painfully stretching my pants. "Is this all for me?"

"Only you." I grabbed her perfect breasts and squeezed, massaging the supple, pliant flesh into different shapes. "Only you, forever."

Sybil's eyes fluttered closed, and she grasped my wrists and seemed to be encouraging me to press harder, grip her tighter.

"Promise?" Her eyes opened, and she bit her lower lip.

"Yes." I could barely gasp out my reply, so fast was my heart beating.

Sybil lifted her skirt until it was rumpled around her

waist. The miniscule undergarment she wore seemed hardly adequate to cover much of anything. She released my wrists and unsnapped the side of her garment, whipping the panties off and across the room. The sweet, musky scent of her nether lips sent me into a near frenzy. I started furiously unbuckling my pants, and Sybil was eagerly helpful in removing them. She lifted her leg in the air, straddled me once more, and slid her dripping wet pussy down over my cock.

She threw her head back and groaned at high volume as my cock buried itself balls deep inside her. Sybil put her hands behind her head and swiveled her hips like an erotic dancer. I was ridden like a boat in a stormy sea, and any thoughts I might have had about just how many times she'd had sex evaporated behind a sea of ecstasy. I quickly decided it didn't matter. Sybil was with me now. Our bodies were conjoined as one, just as our fates had become.

Sybil let out a repetitive, guttural groan each time she slid herself back down my cock. Her cries echoed off the living space walls, growing louder and louder as I struggled to hold myself back. My cock throbbed, swollen and ready to unload its cargo, but I wanted to come at the same time as my love.

Finally, Sybil arched backward on my lap and screamed, her body writhing about as if she had no control over it any longer. I gratefully allowed myself to release, and I pumped her full of my hot load.

Sybil collapsed onto me, leaning her head on my shoulder as we both panted heavily. Our sweat mingled, and I remained inside of her as we recovered until my cock was nearly flaccid.

Then she settled into my lap, and I held her there on the sofa and stroked her soft hair. We uttered those three little words that all couples do, and soon she drifted off to sleep in my arms.

This time, when I watched her sleep, I knew I'd failed to protect her.

The universe had reached out, stabbed her, wounding her in a way we'd never imagined.

But I'd be damned if it happened again.

SYBIL

A rhythmic hum filled the air as our shuttle sailed through the snow-filled skies over Kaster. I sat next to Cazak, holding his massive hand, our fingers intertwined. Our encounter the previous evening had been bittersweet. As much as we had been building the connection between us, it had come on the same day my father had killed himself.

I shook my head, as if to free it of such thoughts. No, my father had not killed himself. The Gorgoxian inside him had forced that fate upon him. Cazak had been quite firm about that point, that those possessed by the Ancient Enemies were no more responsible for their actions than a gun is morally responsible if it's used in a murder.

The Gorgoxian had used my father like a tool, and

then discarded him, like so much trash. I glanced over at the solemnly draped casket which bore my father's remains. At the upcoming funeral, it would remain closed.

My eyes squeezed shut in a vain attempt to stop another deluge of tears. The Gorgoxian had not only stolen my father, it had stolen any chance for me to look at his face and say goodbye. Now when I thought of my father, I could not picture him without seeing an overlay of his hideously fractured skull and dead-eyed stare.

Cazak slipped his arm around my shoulders and I melted into him. The rest of Team Three mostly looked away or feigned blindness, but the big Valorni, Tyehn, did reach out and pat my shoulder in sympathy.

Jalok's knees bounced up and down, his face a mask of barely pent-up rage. The death of my father had hit close to home for him, because of his connection to Dottie. I tried to keep it all in context. Cazak said Jalok had once faced disciplinary action for crippling a group of anti-alienist rioters. Hopefully he would find a legitimate target to unleash his fury upon before he exploded.

Sk'lar stood stoically in the middle aisle, one hand bracing himself on the roof of the cabin. His black eyes remained as inscrutable as ever, but I could see the tension around his mouth. I wondered if his implants were releasing something to help him remain so placid, because Sk'lar also had a human life-mate. He had to have been thinking that she could be vulnerable to the Gorgoxian's influence.

The shuttle lurched to a halt, then descended rapidly toward the windswept tarmac below. The buildings of Kaster came into view through the viewports, but I didn't bother to look. I knew every curve and spire by heart, and had I gazed at the skyline that day, it would have brought me no comfort.

"Damn it all." Jalok peered through the rear viewport. "It looks like there's a huge welcome wagon."

Sk'lar grunted, but I believed he was more than a bit angry.

"We should have figured. Death of a mayor, and all."

His ebon skinned face jerked toward me, as if he'd somehow been disrespectful. I lifted my head from Cazak's shoulder and smiled weakly up at him.

"It's all right, Commander. I've been a wealthy politician's child my whole life. I can handle the attention. Just give me a moment."

"Take all the time you need." Sk'lar locked gazes with Jalok and Navat. They came over for a conference with the commander. Sk'lar spoke in a low tone, but I could make out most of what he said. "I want you two to do a sweep of the crowd. Eject any anti-alienists you come across—gently. We don't want to upset Miss Anatosian more than we have to. Understood?"

The two aliens nodded solemnly. Team Three was sometimes thought of as a group of cowboys, but today they were showing their true colors. These were men of honor, no matter what part of the galaxy they hailed from.

And Cazak was one of them. He held my hand until we reached the top of the ramp, when I gently disengaged from him. It wouldn't do for the mayor's daughter to be seen holding hands with an...

I shook my head. What was I thinking? Cazak looked at me with befuddlement dancing behind his golden eyes as I took his hand again, but I didn't explain. Instead, I threw my shoulders back, held my head high, and adopted a solemn, stoic, but subtly pained expression. It was what would be expected of me during my father's funeral.

The entourage consisted of the entire city council, all turned out to honor my father. Of course, the fact that it was a great opportunity to get exposure in preparation for running for the now empty office of mayor was probably not lost on them either.

They offered their condolences, and their platitudes. I'm sure you've heard it all before. He was a great man, I always considered him a friend, I'm so sorry for your loss.

Loss was a great word, because I felt as if I were moving through the day with half my heart torn asunder. I'd lost my father, and I'd lost a piece of myself, as well.

Their words seemed so inadequate. Some part of me knew that I should be comforted by what they said, but I just felt numb to it all. What good were mere words when invisible monsters were lurking about, waiting to use us until we burned up?

After I made it past the heads of the city, I had to deal with my father's business partners. No doubt all of them were plotting how to swindle me out of my inheritance. I'd never thought much about what I would do after my father died. I didn't want to at that point, either.

I wondered how long they would wait before calling on me with papers to sign. What was the appropriate amount of time for a grieving child? For some reason, the number three popped into my head, but I remembered learning in school that the number three holds arcane significance to the human race, so I might have been way off.

Once past the men of industry in Kaster, I ran into my old partying crowd. I say old, though at the time it had only been days since I'd last spent time with them. In truth, I felt as if I'd aged a hundred years since then.

Still, they were kind, and didn't bat an eye that I was

with Cazak. Perhaps my impassioned speech and subsequent storming off had had the desired effect after all.

But even as the funeral procession marched along to the patch of ground where my father would be laid to rest, I couldn't help but wonder if some of those well-wishers, or holders of power, or captains of industry, were even then under the control of the Gorgoxians. I had begun to think that, perhaps, the Ancient Enemies taking over my father had been some sort of intelligence gathering mission on humanity. Perhaps they were refining their impersonation techniques, so as to give fewer clues to their existence.

My mind kept winding around in the corridors of paranoia, where every veiled look or slight pause in speech was interpreted as a sure sign of Gorgoxian possession. Any one of them could have been possessed, any one.

How could I possibly see any of these people the same way now? That man I danced with at the party, would I soon have to watch as he smashed his own head in? Would the kind alderwoman who patted my cheek and even shed a tear for my father suddenly turn bestial, violent, and attempt to throttle me?

I would have been overwhelmed and pitched forward to huddle in madness on the ground if not for Cazak and the entourage of Team Three. Cazak's hand clenching my own was like a lifeline in a stormy sea, keeping me from drifting away from shore and being swallowed by a massive wave of despair. The Ancient Enemies would not find his mind a fertile place for possession.

I could trust Cazak, and I could trust the aliens around me.

The cotton batting pressed tighter against me, muffling me from the world.

Perhaps I could even trust their loved ones, Dottie, Evie, and the rest, but not completely.

Never completely, not anymore.

No humans could be trusted. Not with the Ancient Enemies around.

The procession ascended a lightly graded hill and reached a place at the top. The Puppet Master had used his vegetation control to pull the earth asunder, forming a smooth fissure in which to lay my father's body. His remains would be used to renew the planet, and help to keep our colony going. It had been my father's wish, before his madness.

Thankfully, no one expected me to speak. I stood near his casket as one official after another made a speech about how wonderful a man Mayor Anatosian had been.

After the third such speaker, I began to long for the funeral to end. I felt terrible for wanting it, as if I were betraying the memory of my father by not giving him his due, but I couldn't control myself.

But I held it together, all the way through the speeches and eulogies and nigh endless pandering to the electorate. Only when the Puppet Master's vines gently lifted my father's casket and lowered it into the fissure did the tears flow.

The fissure closed over, with no sign that it had ever been, but then a twisting vine the size of a man's wrist thrust through the ground where my father had disappeared. The vine wound about in the air, forming a tight serpentine pattern, and my mouth fell open in shock as the image of my father's face appeared.

Using his vines, the Puppet Master had formed a permanent tombstone, a tree which would grow over time but always retain my father's likeness at ground level. The face etched on the tree seemed happy and at peace.

I leaned on Cazak all the way home. Then I draped across him on the sofa and cried some more.

CAZAK

Street lamps cast weak illumination through the windows of Sybil's place. It was somewhere in the early hours of the morning, probably stretching toward dawn. Sybil slept in my arms, her head nestled against my chest. One arm and one leg were thrust out across me, preventing me from moving overly much for fear of waking her.

The funeral had been hard for her, perhaps harder than her father's death. No, scratch that, there was nothing that could be worse than watching someone you loved bludgeon themselves to death, mere puppets on a string subject to the arcane and malevolent whims of unseen incorporeal beings.

I wondered if I, too, would be forced to watch someone I loved forced to kill themselves. Someone like Sybil. Or Dottie, or any of the human friends I'd made on this world.

I knew that I loved the woman I held in my arms, but she had changed irrevocably from her trauma. There was no way to go through an experience such as that, to be subjected to abject, unmitigated horror, and come out the other side unscathed.

Sybil was going to need my help, and Dottie's help, and the help of many others to recover. She seemed warm and ready to accept help from me, and even my cousin Jalok.

But when it came to her interactions with her fellow members of humanity, Sybil had become cold and distant. She remained polite, and could stretch her lips in a smile just as her politician father had done, but I could see the emptiness in her gaze. Sybil's smile no longer reached her eyes when she was around other humans.

I could see why she would feel that way. It had to be hard, knowing that your entire species was vulnerable to being subsumed, consumed, and disposed of like so much flotsam. Worse, I'm certain that Sybil, being a bright woman, had considered the possibility that she herself could succumb to the wiles of the Ancient Enemies.

The chill I'd felt when Fen described the Gorgoxians in the council meeting chamber had never really left, no matter how long I spent in front of a heating unit. My soul had been blasted with the frigid reality that even our greatest foes, the Xathi, might not be the worst thing dwelling in this galaxy.

Crystalline pincers weren't a painless way to go—far from it. And the Xathi could take control of different species, as well, but there were outward signs. Now Sybil would have to get used to a world where any of her species could turn into an enemy at any time, with no outward manifestation.

I wanted to help her. I so desperately wanted to help her, but I had no idea how to go about doing so. My weapons, my training as a soldier, my experiences during fighting, would avail me nothing.

Eventually, in the gray hours of pre-dawn, she stirred and lifted her head to find me already awake.

"Did you sleep at all?" Her voice was thick with slumber still.

"Some. How are you feeling?"

"I don't know." She sighed, and rested her head on my chest once more. "Better, maybe. It's hard to tell. I'm not sure how I feel about anything anymore."

"So, I was thinking."

"Yes?"

"I have to go where my duty takes me, but when I do get to go home, I would like it to be with you, here in Kaster."

"You want to live with me?"

I smiled slightly at the cautious optimism in her voice.

"Of course I do. I love you."

"I love you, too. But it's not going to work, you moving to Kaster."

My face scrunched up in confusion.

"And why is that?"

"Because I'm not staying in Kaster."

I chewed over that particular bombshell. What did she mean, she wasn't going to stay in Kaster?

"Why? Why leave your home?"

"Because, the life that I had here was with my father. Everywhere I look, everywhere I go, I'm reminded of him. And the house just seems, just seems cold and eerie without him living there. There's been too much misery in that place for me to call it home anymore."

"I see. What are you going to do with the house, and your father's business holdings?"

"I've already sold the house and my controlling interest in his companies."

"You have? That's a sudden decision."

"I didn't need any of that weighing me down. Besides, my financial future is quite secure. I won't even have to dip into my trust fund, now that I have resources of my own."

"Where are you going to go?"

"I want to move to Nyheim."

She lifted her head up and locked gazes with me once more.

"If you want to come with me, I would like that, very, very much."

We kissed softly, and then she settled back against my shoulder. She was soft and warm and secure there, lying naked in bed with me. It may not have been paradise, but it was going to have to do.

The next day, we rode with a supply shuttle to Nyheim. Sybil had already arranged for her things to be shipped to Nyheim and held in storage until she found a suitable home for the both of us.

I wanted to be with Sybil. I knew that for a fact, it was engraved on my heart. But I had to ponder the fact that she might never recover from her trauma.

My dream had come true, I was with the beautiful woman of my dreams, but she'd been damaged. I had no qualms about helping her pick up the pieces. I just hoped that I would be up to the task.

As our shuttle began its slow descent toward the skyline of Nyheim, a pair of military craft shot past us, going somewhere in a hurry. For some reason, the sight chilled me to the bone. I had an awful feeling that they weren't just going on a routine patrol.

Sybil and I exchanged glances. I could see in her

somber gaze that we were both thinking the same thing. It was the Gorgoxians. It had to be.

I tried to convince myself that it was a coincidence, or happenstance. After all, there were many reasons why military craft would have to be hastily deployed. It could be more trouble with anti-alien protestors, or maybe some of the strange hybrids Tyehn had fought in the jungles.

But I knew, and so did Sybil. The world had changed, but we just didn't know how much.

Our shuttle dropped toward the tarmac and settled gently on its landing pylons. We headed down the ramp as the supply crew went to work on their cargo.

I was surprised to find Jalok waiting for me, wearing his full combat gear. He had a pack with him, which I recognized as my own, complete with weapons from the armory.

"What's going on?" Sybil squeezed my hand so tightly I feared it would crack.

"You haven't heard?" Jalok's voice held a note of hostility, but I don't think it was directed at me.

"Obviously not. What happened? Obviously, we're being deployed, but why?"

Jalok sighed, and looked off toward the horizon.

"It's Einhiv. We lost the city."

"What?" My jaw hung slack as my heart started to pound in my chest. "We lost it? The whole city?'

"That's what I said, isn't it?"

"How? What happened? Why didn't security forces take action?"

Jalok's jaw worked silently before he replied.

"Because the security forces were the ones to take the city. It's the Gorgoxians. They've taken over everyone with any power or authority in Einhiv, and probably most of the general populace, as well. We assume that any nonhuman denizens have been captured or killed."

Einhiv.

Gone.

Just like that, and without a shot fired.

We were in dire straits. Sybil and I clung to each other, until Jalok pointed out our transport was awaiting us.

The new war had begun.

The war that Fen said would make the Xathi invasion look like a schoolyard brawl.

And I had more to lose than ever.

SYBIL

It was early spring. The snow was starting to melt, but weather reports said that we were in line for one more massive snowstorm before winter was officially over. The city of Nyheim was not Kaster, and at the moment, that was a good thing.

Kaster held too many memories of my mother and father for me. I had been able to handle staying there after mom died because dad was there. But, now? No. I didn't want anything to do with the place. Not for a long while.

Over the last month, I'd bought a place to live, Cazak had moved in, and Dottie was trying to help me find things to do. I appreciated her concern and her love, but I don't want to do anything. If I did something that got me into contact with other people, then I'd get to know them, and that would mean that, if and when they were taken over by the Gorgoxians, or whatever the hell those things were that killed my father, I would have to deal with that again.

And that was something I wanted nothing to do with, if possible.

Keeping Dottie and some of the other human women as part of my life was already enough of a risk. Knowing that Cazak was a soldier and could potentially die any time he went out, that was enough of a worry. I didn't need to add the nonstop wonder of whether or not someone around me was going to be taken over added to my life.

Despite the fact that it was already there. Any time I went out of the house, I had to wonder if one of the people walking down the street, or handing me my food at the deli, or stocking the shelves at the store, was about to turn and go apeshit crazy.

I liked that phrase. We didn't have apes here on Ankau, but my father's digital library had lots of information about Earth and its animals. I had grown up wanting to become a zoologist when I was little. Mom getting sick and dad going into politics changed all of that. I still liked animals, though.

And apes, when they were pushed to a point of going berserk, they *looked* as though they were crazy. Hence, when someone lost their minds and did things that looked ridiculously crazy, people said they went apeshit crazy. It was fun thinking back to those things.

Other than Cazak, his cousin Jalok, Dottie, and my memories and my study of animals, nothing really was fun anymore.

I walked out of the kitchen and into one of the rooms that Cazak had turned into his office. He had installed computers and systems so he could keep track of things that were happening. Despite his nonstop insistence on simply being a regular soldier, he really was an exemplary soldier that would be a fantastic officer.

"Hey there, shweethahrt," he said as I walked into his office. He tried, desperately, to imitate the accent from one of my old-time movies from Earth, but he just couldn't get the inflection right. I smiled at him, though. He could butcher it every single time and I wouldn't care. He was mine and I knew that we loved one another, and that he wouldn't be taken away from me by some mystical enemy that stole people's minds.

"Hi, baby," I said, a smile on my face. "I noticed you didn't eat breakfast. Again."

He shrugged at me, but at least he had the grace and dignity enough to look a little ashamed. "Yeah, sorry. I was going to eat, when some of the alarms went off in here."

"Uh-huh. And what did your magical alarms tell you today?"

The look of disappointment on his face almost told me before he did. "Einhiv."

"More people?" I asked.

He nodded and turned to one of the computers on his left, my right. He pointed at it. "See all of this right here?" he asked, showing me nearly four dozen streams of yellow heading into the city of Einhiv. "That's every single person that's traveled from various places around the continent and to Einhiv."

"But how many people? Those are just lines."

"Oh. Sorry." He clicked a few buttons and the lines were suddenly dots. Hundreds of dots. I knew my eyes were wide in disbelief because, when he turned to look back at me, he nodded in the same disbelieving state that I felt. "Yeah. We're talking hundreds of people, and we don't even know who they all are."

"Wow," I breathed. Then I looked at him and gave him my you-need-to-listen-to-my-words look. "Breakfast. Now. Let's go." I turned away from him and made my way back towards the kitchen. "Now," I repeated when I didn't hear his chair move.

"Yes, dear," he said in resignation, but I knew he was teasing. "You know this is bad news, right?"

"I do," I said. They weren't my friends. They weren't my family. I didn't have family anymore. Well, I had

Cazak and Dottie, but they were the family I had chosen. But what had happened to my father could happen to the families of all those people on the pad. Thinking about that day in the detention center made me realize what I had to do.

"Seriously?"

I turned around and looked at him. "Look. My mother died years ago due to what we now know as NOX. My father died a month ago due to some ancient being that takes over bodies. Other people are losing themselves to those people. I get it. It sucks. It's horrible. It's terrible. And I never realized just how dangerous they were. I want you to let me help you. I have considerable resources and I've seen up close what they can do. But right now, my only care at this moment is whether or not you eat breakfast." I turned around and walked around the island to the refrigeration unit. "And let me fill you in on a *tiny* little secret, my love. If you don't eat breakfast, I'm going to be really angry with you. *That's* what I care about."

I stared at him, daring him to argue with me. He didn't.

"You're right. I need to eat. Okay. What do we attempt to cook this morning before we give up and head to the diner?"

"Ha, you're hilarious. I'm happy to tell you that I'm

actually pretty good at biscuits and gravy. I'll teach you."

"Yeah?" he smiled. "I'd like that."

We spent the next hour making, and then eating, biscuits and gravy. I made my mother's famous cheese biscuits while I walked him through making the gravy. He was pretty good at it.

After breakfast, he went back into his office and looked at things some more. He really was dedicated to his work, just like an officer. It was his day off, and instead of spending the time with me, he was looking over reports and things. Yeah, he was officer material, he just didn't want to admit it.

"Why are you working?" I asked when I was done with the dishes.

"Sorry. Didn't mean to be. I just wanted to check on some things and I guess I got caught up."

"Come on, leave work alone. I want to do something, just the two of us. And, no, not that," I added quickly before he could make a quip about sleeping together, again. You would figure he would have been worn out, but I guess Skotans have unbelievable drive and stamina.

"Ah, okay," he said, dejected. But he smiled. "Are you sure you're doing okay?"

"Why wouldn't I be?"

"Well," he said as he leaned back in his chair. "You're

not exactly the same girl that I met. You're not as open and outgoing anymore."

"I have to reason to be," I answered. I hated this conversation. I had already had this with him, in my mind, a few dozen times and it never went well. "But I realized something when you showed me your pad about everyone going to Einhiv."

"What's that?"

"There's something that will make me feel a whole hell of a lot better," I said.

"Oh, really?" Cazak asked. "What is it?"

I paused for a moment.

"Revenge," I said simply.

He got up from his chair and came over, putting his hands on my shoulders and rubbing them. "I'm worried about you. I know that this last month has been rough, and different, but I just want to make sure that you're okay. That's all."

"I know that," I answered as I got up on my tiptoes and kissed him. I figured that if his lips were busy kissing mine, he wouldn't ask me questions. "But I'm fine. I really am. I just need to realize that for the longest time, I had no direction in my life. I have that now. And I want to avenge my father. I want to make those ancient bastards pay for what they did."

He kissed me again. "Okay. Okay." We kissed a couple more times before he finally pulled back, smiled, and asked, "So, what do you want to do now that you know you want vengeance?"

"First, I'm going to read and learn everything I can. I'm going to talk to this Puppet Master. I'm going to prepare myself. I'm going to beg and plead you and your general to help you and get access to what you guys know." I paused for the right words.

I'd been thinking about this, over and over in my mind, but saying it aloud made it real.

And saying it to Cazak made it right.

Safe.

"I have more resources, more contacts, than I realized. Every person who was at my father's funeral. Everyone who's been affected by these Ancient Enemies."

I kissed his cheek. "We've been relying on you and the *Vengeance* crew for so much. But it's time we came together, those of us who might not have science backgrounds or obvious skills. We'll find a way to help, and I'm going to make it happen."

"You sound determined," he said. "And I'm a bit worried."

I smiled at him and shook my head. "This is war, Cazak. And I've just been made into a soldier." I leaned back, thought about my father for a moment, then put it aside. "I always wanted a purpose, something that would use my position to help people." I wound my fingers in his. "And now I have it."

"You've got more than that," he answered. "You've got me."

I snuggled into his chest, listened to his heartbeat, felt the strong arms that wrapped around me.

A strength that would never hold me back, never put constraints around me.

But it would lift me up, make me even stronger.

"And you've got me," I answered, tilting my face up to meet his lips with my own. "Forever."

LETTER FROM ELIN

Sybil's had a rough road, but you know Cazak will be there to keep her focused. And she'll always remind him that he's the most handsome man (or alien) on the planet to her.

I couldn't resist playing with the idea of how one of the "pretty people" would handle this new world. And the perfect mate had to be someone who was convinced he was too ugly to love.

It was a fun plan, but then Sybil and Cazak became their own people, and not just my random notion. And I love what they've decided to do with the story :)

Coming up next? Navat! Keep reading for a sneak peak, and I'll catch you next time!

XOXO,

Elin

PLEASE DON'T FORGET TO LEAVE A REVIEW!

Readers rely on your opinions, and your review can help others decide on what books they read. Make sure your opinion is heard and leave a review where you purchased this book!

Don't miss a new release! You can sign up for release alerts at both Amazon and Bookbub:

bookbub.com/authors/elin-wyn
amazon.com/author/elinwyn

For a free short story, opportunities for advance review copies, release news and the occasional cat picture, please join the newsletter!

https://elinwynbooks.com/newsletter-signup/

And don't forget the Facebook group, where I post sneak peeks of chapters and covers!

https://www.facebook.com/groups/ElinWyn/

NAVAT: SNEAK PEEK

Navat
"You know what angers me?" I grumbled as I stalked down the corridors.

"What?" Sakev asked me.

"I've done this before. The humans have a phrase for it. Experiencing the same moment over and over again?"

"Déjà vu," a voice piped up from behind me. I looked over my shoulder to see Amira, a spunky human and the sister-in-law of Strike Team One's leader, Vrehx. Since Jeneva gave birth, she's taken a step back from her duties in General Rouhr's organization. I supposed Amira had picked up some of the slack in her sister's place, though I hadn't talked to her much.

She seemed okay. Tough as nails and determined as

skrell. Then again, all the humans had to be tough as nails now, even the gentle ones like Dr. Parr. Their planet- our planet now- couldn't seem to catch a break.

"Déjà vu," I repeated, testing the strange syllabus on my tongue.

"It means *already seen* in French," Amira explained. "You literally feel like you've already seen and done this before."

"That's exactly it," I muttered. "And it pisses me off."

"Elaborate," Sakev jerked his chin in my direction.

"Remember that whole deal with the Xathi hybrids?" I said. "I feel like I've already gone through the human population and cleansed it of an invasive species. I'm not thrilled about having to do this all over again. What was the point of doing it all the first time if we're right back where we started?"

"It's not exactly the same," Amira offered. "For one thing, the hybridism antidote we concocted does jack shit for this new type of possession. Xathi hybridism operated like a plague, a virus. This is a brain thing. A weird brain thing."

"Is that the technical term?" I smirked.

"Shut up," Amira chuckled. "This isn't my field of expertise. I'm learning as I go, just like everyone else here."

"Fair enough," I shrugged. "Do you ever get sick of all this?"

"Of course," she scoffed. "You think I want to be dealing with Xathi, Puppet Masters, and whatever this new fresh hell is?"

"Gorgoxians," Sakev said. "The anti-alien dickheads are calling them Gorgos for short. I hate those fuckers but it's catchy."

"Which fuckers?" I asked. "The anti-alien dickheads or the Gorgos?"

"Both."

"I second that," Amira quipped. "The last year has been one never-ending migraine."

"Even the part where you fell in love?" Sakev teased.

"Especially the part where I fell in love," Amira winked. "Speaking of love, Dax said he'll be along to help out shortly. He's in a meeting right now."

"Do you think we'll need him?" I asked. "Sakev and I have more than enough muscle between the two of us."

"Theoretically, we won't need him," Amira explained. "However, when have things ever gone according to theory for us?"

"I think it happened once a few weeks ago," I joked. "But seriously, any idea what we're dealing with today?"

"The scouting group hasn't checked in yet," she said.

"Isn't that concerning?"

"I'm choosing to believe no news is good news." The nervous glint in her eyes didn't escape my notice.

"When has that ever been the case for us?" I asked, instantly regretting my words.

"Never," Amira admitted. "But anything is possible, right? This past year has surely proved that."

"Without a doubt," Sakev agreed.

We've reached one of the newly renovated holding cells. It'd been reinforced five times over since it was redone. Right now, it stood empty.

"Now what?"

"Now we play the waiting game," Amira sighed. "I'll try to get the scout team on the radio."

"Be cautious," Sakev warned. "If they're closing in on a target, a radio call might give away their position."

"Good point," Amira tapped her chin. "I'll try to get their navigation location on a datapad."

Amira walked off in search of a datapad. I turned to Sakev.

"I'm still pissed off."

"When are you not?" Sakev joked.

"I've been pissed off since I joined the Valorni ranks," I said.

"Trust me, I'm aware," Sakev laughed. "Do you regret it, though?"

"I don't think so," I said after a moment of consideration. "I mean, we've landed in a shit situation here. I know not everyone thinks so, especially the lucky ones who found mates," I gave Sakev a pointed look. He grinned back at me.

"You jealous?" He asked.

"Not exactly," I shrugged. "I'm jealous that some have found reasons to make staying here worthwhile. I don't need a mate thrown into this mess, though. It'll only complicate things."

"Let me put it this way, what would you be doing if you weren't here?"

"Probably doing the same thing somewhere else," I laughed dryly. "The Xathi are still wreaking havoc elsewhere in the galaxies. Odds are, I'd be doing the same thing I'm doing now only without the support of Strike Teams and a good General. I'd be a civilian."

"There you go." Sakev clapped his hands together. "You're not pissed about being a soldier. You're just pissed off. It's part of your personality."

I laughed genuinely this time.

"Thanks for the pep talk. You should start charging for them."

"I know, right?"

"I got something!" Amira rushed into the room, datapad in hand. "The scout team is heading back."

"Did they get a Gorgo?"

"I think so," she replied. "And we shouldn't call them that. They're still people."

"They're husks," I said flatly. "The Gorgo is the one steering the ship if you catch my meaning."

"Still, it skeeves me out," Amira shuddered. "They're people. When the new subject arrives, we should treat them as such."

"Only if they act as such," I said decisively.

"You're an asshole, Navat. Has anyone ever told you that?" Amira grinned.

"Many times," I smirked. "What kind of prep do we need to do for our new guest? Food and water bowls?"

"Please, never reproduce," Amira jabbed.

"I have great paternal instincts, for your information," I shot back.

"I'll believe that when I see it. Get ready. The scout team is back."

Amira grabbed the radio from Sakev's belt and clicked to the correct frequency.

"Talk to me. What do we have?"

"Single subject," a staticky voice came through. "Displaying no signs of aggression. Minimal signs of awareness."

"You're sure it's an occupied host?" She asked, wincing on the words.

That was the tricky thing about the Gorgos. They tended to overload their hosts. We'd noticed they've gotten better at abandoning a host before a host dies, but that wasn't a good thing. Vacated hosts were... screwy, for lack of better word.

So far, the vacated hosts we'd observed were nothing like they were before the Gorgo invaded their minds. Best case scenario, it was like they were drugged or in some kind of haze. Worst case was a host gone mad. We hadn't found a way to reverse that yet. The ladies up in the labs were working on it night and day but they had almost nothing to go off.

Enter the scouts.

We'd all had a turn on the scout teams but some were a better fit than others. I was better suited to the second phase: dealing with the subject.

Now that Einhiv was basically a Gorgo colony, the scouts had a good hunting ground to pick up affected humans.

The front doors to the holding facility were kicked open and a small group of heavily armored scouts entered the room. Each had a hold on a human woman who looked far too pale for comfort. There was a telltale glazed look in her eyes. She wouldn't even move her feet. They were dragging behind her. I could see that the scouts were doing whatever they could not to injure her in the transport process but she didn't seem aware of what was happening around her.

She didn't put up a fight as she was put in the

holding cell. Two scouts gently placed her in a chair before taking their leave.

"She's all yours," one of the scouts, a human male, nodded to us. We didn't have many human volunteers. It was nice to see one on our side.

"Thanks," Amira nodded back. She looked at the woman in the holding cell. "Can you tell us your name?"

The woman said nothing. She didn't even blink.

"We're going to run a few tests on you," Amira explained. "They aren't supposed to hurt so if you feel any pain, you need to let me know immediately. Can you do that?"

No response.

"Can we even test on her like this?" I asked.

"We don't have a choice. Every ounce of information we can get is helpful."

"But will she be able to tell us if something is wrong?"

"I'm not sure," Amira frowned.

"That's some kind of ethical violation isn't it?" Sakev wondered out loud.

"We're ethically obligated to protect the women, but not the Gorgo. If the Gorgo is present inside her, we're obligated to test on it."

"I understand what you mean about those migraines, Amira," I groaned.

With the anti-alien presence still strong in most of the cities, General Rouhr and Mayor Vidia wanted us to take extra precautions with everything we did. The last thing we needed was to be accused of treating people inhumanely.

After everything we've done to keep the human population safe, it was ridiculous that we still didn't have their full trust.

Leena breezed in, scrolling through her notes. Dr. Parr followed closely behind.

"Are we ready to start testing?"

"I can't verify the presence of a Gorgo," Amira said.

"We'll start with the gentlest test first," Leena decided. "She shouldn't feel a thing. Gorgo or no Gorgo."

"Works for me," Amira shrugged.

The reinforced walls and windows in the holding cell weren't the only renovations. This cell, in particular, was set up for testing. All of the scanners and other fancy technical stuff was already installed. Leena could run tests without going into the holding cell.

"Running test one: Thermo scan," Leena spoke into a recorder. She pressed a few buttons on her datapad.

We'd figured out that Gorgo's affected the body temperature of the host. An occupied human's temperature ran over one hundred degrees.

Machinery whirled. All of our eyes were fixed on the woman. She still hadn't reacted to anything around her.

Once the thermal scanner fired up, that all changed.

She went ballistic. She screamed and thrashed, leaping out of her seat to slam herself into the reinforced walls which, thankfully, held.

"Should we turn it off?" Amira asked.

"No." Leena's gaze went steely. "This is a new reaction. We have to observe."

"She's going to break her face," I said.

"We can release tranq gas if it gets too serious," Leena said. "Dr. Parr is here for a reason, as well."

The woman turned to us. It was difficult to explain, but it looked as if there was a second face beneath her actual face.

The Gorgo.

The woman let out a howl. The second face disappeared. She collapsed to the floor, still as a stone.

ALESSA

"Are you sure you want to do it yourself?"

"Are you kidding?" I laughed as I pulled the harness up my legs. Fastening it around my waist, I put the locking carabiners in place and ran my hands across the rope to ensure it was properly tied onto the rappelling structure. "Of course I want to do it." My foreman, Andorian, looked at me with a disapproving glance, both hands on his hips as he shook his head.

"Most engineers I know are glad to remain behind their desk, you know?" Grabbing my hand, he helped me over the bridge steel railings. He didn't look too happy about the fact that I was doing something he saw as being part of his job, but he knew better than to complain.

"I'm not like most engineers you know," I threw right back at him. I lowered my center of gravity until my body was parallel with the Sauma river, a mass of turbulent waters 800 feet below, and pressed my feet against the pillar in front of me. Winking at Andorian, I eased the hold I had on the rope and allowed my body to go down, my knees locked as I made my descent.

Not really a fan of heights, I kept my gaze on the pillar and my feet. I could hear the water rippling from underneath me, a steady breeze whipping at the hair that escaped from my helmet, but I just ignored it all and kept on going down. Andorian was right—most engineers would leave a task such as this to their underlings—but I never really cared to be a pencil pusher. I liked being in the middle of the action, even if that meant facing my fear of heights. Besides, being that I was younger than most engineers in charge of such big projects, I had to prove my mettle to the crew.

"Alright," I muttered once I had dropped almost 200 feet, gripping the rope tightly so that I'd stop in place. Narrowing my eyes, I looked at the bolts in the temporary steel frame supporting the pillar. Someone had messed up, it seemed—the steel bolts they had put in place weren't the ones I had ordered to be used, and that meant we would have to replace this entire structure. That, of course, would translate as an inevitable delay.

"Pull me up," I cried out, looking up the pillar. From where I was, I couldn't see any of my workers, but I knew they could hear me. Except it seemed that they couldn't. I remained hanging there for a couple of seconds before reaching for the radio in my belt. Careful not to let go of the rope, I turned the radio on. "What the hell are you doin' up there, Andorian? Pull me up. I've figured out the problem already."

Again, silence.

I got nothing but the crackle of radio static.

The damn assholes were already probably lost in conversation, trying to arrange another nightly gathering of poker. As much as I liked them, I had to keep on top of them at all times, or else nothing would ever get done. Not that I had any reason to complain— aside from this minor screw-up, everything was going perfectly. Sure, we'd have to ask for a one week extension on our deadline, but that wasn't anything to worry about. Months of delays were perfectly natural in jobs of this nature, especially with all the logistic mess this damn continent turned into after the war.

"Andorian?" I insisted. "Do you copy?"

Exhaling sharply, I realized I would have to hoist myself up. Not an easy task, but I would gladly do it just so I could skin Andorian alive. I couldn't believe he got distracted and left me hanging while knowing that—

"Shit," I cried out, the rope losing some of its tension and sending me down a dozen feet. My feet lost their grip on the pillar, and I balanced from the rope like a sack of potatoes someone had slung over the bridge. "What the hell are you assholes doin' up there?" I cried out while trying to grab the radio. My fingers were clammy and, as I tightened them around the plastic, it slipped from my fingers and the radio dropped into the river below.

I felt a knot form in my throat as I followed the radio with my gaze, nothing but a black dot being swallowed up by the rabid foam of a merciless river. I always tried not to look down when rappelling, but this time it was unavoidable—I was staring straight down at the abyss.

My heart thrashed inside my chest, and adrenaline started coursing through my veins like battery acid. It was hard to breathe, let alone think straight. "You got this, Alessa, you got this," I repeated over and over again, a stupid little mantra I hoped would calm me down. Foot by foot, I started making the climb up. My body was covered in sweat, my drenched clothes sticking to my body, but I kept going all the same.

"Hang on, Alessa," I finally heard a familiar voice cry out, and I looked up to see Andorian peeking over the railings. From the distance I couldn't really make out his face, but judging by his tone of voice I could tell he was panicking. What the hell was going on up there?

My body relaxed as I started feeling the pull of the rope once more, and I suddenly went up the pillar faster and faster. I didn't even care that the rope was biting into my ungloved hands. All I cared about was making it over the edge, safe and sound.

"I got you," Andorian muttered once I was within reach. Taking my hand, he hoisted me over the railings and I immediately collapsed on the floor, exhaustion finally taking over me. I sat on the ground, elbows resting on my knees, and I took deep breaths as I waited for the adrenaline to run its course.

"What the hell just happened?" I finally asked, somehow managing to push me up to my feet. Raking one hand over my face, I looked straight at Andorian, and my stomach lurched the moment I saw the deep creases on his forehead. He was my foreman because he *never* panicked, nor did he stress over things. He was the kind of man you could count on when things got tough, and he always kept his head over his shoulders. Now, though, there was fear etched deep on his face.

"I don't know, Alessa, I really don't," he whispered, looking down at his feet as he spoke. Running one hand through his thinning hair, he finally looked into my eyes and pursed his lips. "They just up and left, the lot of 'em."

"What do you mean they up and left?"

"See for yourself," he continued, waving with his hand at one end of the bridge. I spun around and, shading my eyes from the sun with one hand, watched as dozens of workers dragged their feet toward some point in the distance. They were ambling in an discoordinate way, the soles of their heavy boots dragging across the concrete, and they didn't seem to be paying attention to anything on their way.

There were other workers there, handling the machinery on the clearing by the end of the bridge, and they just shuffled out of the way as the group of runaway workers made their way past them.

"It happened all of a sudden," Andorian said, his voice low. "A few were handling the ropes, others were just milling around, and then..." He hesitated for a moment, shifted his weight from one foot to the other, and breathed out. "I don't know what came over them. They just dropped their tools, all at the same time, and started walking out."

"All of them?"

"Almost all of them," he replied. "Some, like me, kept our wits about us. But the rest of them just lost it. I tried talking to them, shouting their names, and I even stood in their way and tried to stop them. They wouldn't budge. They just kept on walking and walking, almost as if there's something in the jungle calling for them."

I opened my mouth to say something but, in the end, just remained silent. Whatever was going on wasn't normal, that was for sure.

"What should we do?" Andorian asked me.

"Let 'em go," I said, watching as the group of dazed workers kept on walking through the clearing and disappeared out into the jungle, their discoordinated bodies swallowed up by the thick green foliage. Wherever they were going, it wouldn't be safe for any of the other workers to follow. "We have no idea what's going on, and I'm not going to risk the rest of our crew." Taking a deep breath, I straightened my back and started walking down the bridge.

"Where are you going?" Andorian asked, and I didn't even bother looking back at him to reply.

"What do you think?" I threw back at him, doing my best not to let anxiety spread its wings inside me. "I'm going to call this in."

. . .

Navat

THE WOMAN only raised more questions and created more cause for concern the longer we observed her. After the Thermal test, she essentially went comatose.

Weird thing was, her eyes were open.

"We have to go in," Dr. Parr insisted. "She needs help."

"Can we verify that the Gorgo is gone?" Sakev asked.

"I think I saw it leave," I said.

"But can you be sure?"

"Are any of us sure of anything in this situation?" I fired back.

"That's my point," Sakev exclaimed. "If a Gorgo decides to use one of us as a host, our entire operation is fucked."

"We can't just leave her there," Amira insisted. "She's our only shot at understanding what just happened."

"Grab the gas masks," Dr. Parr said decisively.

"Will that help?" Amira lifted a brow.

"I don't know but it'll make me feel better. Leena?"

Leena nodded and retrieved two gas masks from the emergency supply cupboard on the far end of the room.

"Grab a third one," I called to her. "I'm going in with you."

"Let me go," Sakev insisted. "Evie's my mate. I should be in there protecting her."

"That's why you shouldn't," I argued. "I can be more objective in this situation than you can."

"He's got a point," Amira pursed her lips.

"If I'm in there, I need someone monitoring readings from out here." Dr. Parr tapped the top of her datapad. "I'll need both hands when I'm in here. Sakev, I've taught you how to read this kind of stuff."

Dr. Parr flipped the datapad around to reveal charts filled with jagged lines, rows of numbers, and a slew of other stuff I didn't understand.

"I need you to tell me what's happening on her insides while I'm in there," she said.

"Can do," Sakev nodded.

Leena tossed me a gas mask.

"I hope this does something," I muttered and I slipped it on.

"We don't know how Gorgos infect their hosts. Could be an airborne virus type of deal," Leena said.

"That's enough for me. Let's do this."

I opened the door to the reinforced cell. If the woman on the floor was aware of the movement, she didn't react. Her blank gaze was fixed on the ceiling above. She stared right into one of the fluorescent lights, unblinking.

"Ma'am?" Dr. Parr called out. "I'm a doctor. I'm here to help you. Can you tell me if you feel any pain?"

To no one's surprise, the woman didn't answer.

"She looks dehydrated," Evie said, tilting her head to one side. The three of us looked creepy as skrell standing here with the gas masks over our faces. We're probably the last thing that woman wanted to see.

"Maybe the Gorgo's don't know what a human host body needs," Leena said. "That could be why they abandon their hosts so quickly."

"I don't think so," I frowned.

Leena turned her steely gaze on me.

"Elaborate."

"The Gorgo's are strong enough to suck the life out of things like the Puppet Master, right?" I said. "The Puppet Master is strong, too strong to be taken down by brute force alone. The Gorgo's have to be strategic in the way they suck the life out of the other Puppet Masters which implies they're capable of studying and learning about their hosts."

"But did the Gorgo's actively inhabit the Puppet Master's family?" Leena asked.

"I don't know," I admitted.

"None of us know anything," Dr. Parr sighed.

She knelt down beside the woman and checked her pulse.

"She's alive but her pulse is weak," she said. "She really needs fluids. Can we have some brought in?"

"I'll make the call," Sakev said from the outside.

"Can you call Sk'lar in here as well?" I asked. "I think he'll want to see this."

Sakev nodded and spoke rapidly into his radio.

"Help me," a rasping voice said. I turned my attention back to the woman.

"Help me," the voice came again. It had to be from the woman, it couldn't have been from anyone else. Yet, her lips weren't moving. Her eyes showed no sign of awareness.

"Is that her?"

"I think so," Dr. Parr said, looking just as perplexed as I felt.

"She looks...drier," Leena said.

"Hosting the Gorgo took too much out of her," Dr. Parr's voice sounded thick. "It's desperately trying to make up for the depleted resources but it's not working."

"And her mouth isn't moving when she speaks because?" I prompted.

"I can't help you there," Dr. Parr clicked her tongue. "Maybe we can ask her when she comes around."

"I don't think that's going to happen," Leena said softly.

I looked back at the woman. Somehow, she looked

even more vacant than she had a second ago. I knew she was gone.

"What a shame," I murmured.

"Let's get her into the medical wing for an autopsy," Leena sighed heavily. Dr. Parr said nothing.

"You wanted to see me, Navat?" Sk'lar's voice took my attention off the dead woman. The rest of Strike Team Three followed him into the room. A nice surprise.

I exited the holding cell while Sakev helped Leena bring in a stretcher. Dr. Parr knelt beside the woman. Her lips moved but I couldn't hear her speech. I wondered what she was saying.

"I wanted you to witness this subject first hand," I said. "But there's no point. She just died."

"Oh," Sk'lar's face fell. "What killed her?"

"I think it was the force of the Gorgo leaving her body," I said. "Though, we still haven't verified that she was a host. We didn't get a chance to verify anything, actually."

"Did you observe anything unusual?"

"She was calm while she was brought in," I reported. "She didn't fight the scouts. She only acted up when we started the thermal test and even then, her aggression didn't seem to be directed at us."

Sk'lar furrowed his brow.

"That's the most non-invasive test. Why would she react so negatively to it?"

"I have a theory," Amira piped up.

"By all means." Sk'lar made a sweeping gesture with his hand.

"Assuming she was infested with a Gorgo," Amira started, "I think it knew what we were doing."

"You mean, it knew we were testing for its presence?" Sk'lar asked.

"Exactly. It didn't freak out until we started actively searching for it," she continued. "I think it started forcing the host to hurt herself in an attempt to make us stop testing."

Sk'lar looked to me.

"Makes sense to me," I shrugged.

"That goes against known Gorgo behavior," Cazak said thoughtfully.

"What little we have, that is," Jalok added.

"I've never seen a Gorgo fight to avoid detection, let alone fight to keep a specific host," Sk'lar said. "They usually discard a host soon after inhabiting it. They don't take care to avoid detection."

"Maybe there was something specific about this woman." I gestured to the body leaving the room on a stretcher. I didn't even know her name. I shook off a wave of disgust for the Gorgos. "Maybe they aren't just taking over the bodies, they're also harvesting knowledge."

"We don't have anything that supports that theory," Amira said.

"Except we do," I countered. "All of those scientists out in the Sika Jungle were taken over by Gorgos and were used for something specific. It's a fair bet the Gorgo sought those scientists out."

Amira narrowed her eyes.

"What did you say your background was?"

"Construction," I answered. "Why?"

"You're wasted in that field," she said. "Should've been a detective."

"A what?"

"A human puzzle solver," she clarified. "One that catches criminals."

"Sounds boring."

Amira snorted.

"Do you think we could compile a list of humans with useful traits?" Jalok asked. "We could be proactive and put those people into protective custody."

"Everyone on this planet has some kind of useful trait," Amira said. "We're a young colony world. We aren't established enough for people to sit around in their summer homes and do nothing. Everyone here still pulls their weight in some way or another."

"That might be why they narrowed in on this

planet," I said. "If there are other Puppet Masters out there, why is ours such a big draw? The accomplished human population is likely a factor."

"But to what end? Sk'lar asked. "How much can the Gorgo's expect to accomplish if they keep draining and discarding their hosts?"

"Maybe they're taking the knowledge even when the body shuts down," Tyhen suggested.

"That's possible," Sk'lar nodded. "Prevention should be our first priority, nonetheless."

"What about extraction?" I asked. "We can prevent all we want but we still can't narrow down how the Gorgo's get into their hosts. We ran a thermal test on that woman and the Gorgo fled. Surely, that means something?"

"Yes, but it killed her when it fled," Sk'lar replied. "We can't let that happen to everyone who ends up a host."

"We need another subject to run tests on." Amira gnawed on the inside of her cheek. "Until then, we're just running on theories and making guesses."

"What else is new?" I laughed. "We've been running on theories and educated guesses since the *Vengeance* smashed into this rock. We should be old pros at this by now."

"Glad you can still find something to laugh about, Navat," Sk'lar gave me a stern look but it didn't knock the smile off my face. If I didn't find the humor in situations like this, I'd be a seething pile of anger at all hours. No one wanted that, least of all me.

I'd gotten good at finding the humor in even the bleakest of situations. I'd had an entire lifetime to perfect the art of it. I wasn't about to stop now.

GET NAVAT NOW!

HTTPS://ELINWYNBOOKS.COM/CONQUERED-WORLD-ALIEN-ROMANCE/

DON'T MISS THE STAR BREED!

Given: Star Breed Book One

When a renegade thief and a genetically enhanced mercenary collide, space gets a whole lot hotter!

Thief Kara Shimsi has learned three lessons well - keep her head down, her fingers light, and her tithes to the syndicate paid on time.

But now a failed heist has earned her a death sentence - a one-way ticket to the toxic Waste outside the dome. Her only chance is a deal with the syndicate's most ruthless enforcer, a wolfish mountain of genetically-modified muscle named Davien.

The thought makes her body tingle with dread-or is it heat?

Mercenary Davien has one focus: do whatever is necessary to get the credits to get off this backwater mining colony and back into space. The last thing he wants is a smart-mouthed thief - even if she does have the clue he needs to hunt down whoever attacked the floating lab he and his created brothers called home.

Caring is a liability. Desire is a commodity. And love could get you killed.

https://elinwynbooks.com/star-breed/

ABOUT THE AUTHOR

I love old movies – *To Catch a Thief, Notorious, All About Eve* — and anything with Katherine Hepburn in it. Clever, elegant people doing clever, elegant things.

I'm a hopeless romantic.

And I love science fiction and the promise of space.

So it makes perfect sense to me to try to merge all of those loves into a new science fiction world, where dashing heroes and lovely ladies have adventures, get into trouble, and find their true love in the stars!